Chumped
Collection

ALEXEI AULD

DEDICATION

For every Percy Winkler struggling and surviving.

ACKNOWLEDGMENTS

This story would not have been possible without my inner Percy.

1

"PERCY! COME HERE. NOW."

Lance didn't look like himself. Pressed against a door. Disheveled. Desperate. Demanding help. It made Percy's earlobes tingle.

Percy zipped up his pants, fresh from a hearty and productive bathroom visit. His nose whistled as he inhaled, bolstered in his never-ending battle with congestion.

"Morning, Lance. What's going—"

In one fluid motion, Lance grabbed Percy with his left hand, opened the door with his right hand, and tossed Percy into the room.

Percy landed flat on his back. Felt sticky tobacco juice showering his face, invading his stuffy sinus. He rose to his knees, face full of crotch.

"Lemonjelo, I mean Mr. Jermajesty, how can I help you, sir?"

Lemonjelo was a former NFL player ejected from the league for cheating on a urine test with the "Piss-Pass 2.0", a device that looked like a penis and secreted a false negative urine sample. As disgusting as it seemed, it was quite the sensation in organized sports leagues. Lemonjelo had sued the manufacturers of the Piss-Pass for false advertising.

"If it worked the way it was supposed to, I'd still be playing for the Giants."

And the arbitrator had agreed with him, thanks to the efforts of unheralded nebbish Percy Winkler, supervising partner Dick Bacon, and their law firm, Canker Shore. Lemonjelo was pleased with the outcome. Just not with the legal bill.

When Lemonjelo had arrived at the firm an hour earlier, Lance had locked him in a conference room. Lance couldn't be bothered with mundane tasks like billing, so he'd left to work on other matters and forgotten Lemonjelo. With only a door separating Lance from walking roid rage, he hadn't known what to do.

Percy, locked in a room with Lemonjelo, didn't either.

"The fuck is up with the doors around here?"

"I don't follow you, sir."

"That prick Lance told me to wait in here and next thing I know, the door jams."

"Sorry about that, sir."

"Yeah, well, fuck that. This is what I came here for." Lemonjelo whipped out a legal bill and jabbed at it. "What kind of shit is this?"

Percy looked at the bill and replied, "Fifty cents a copy, sir."

"Fifty cents? It only costs a dime at Kinkos."

"I know, sir, but they don't have the expertise to handle the paperwork."

"Expertise? All they do is make copies all day long. I'd call that expertise."

"Not legal expertise, sir."

"What kind of legal expertise do you need to make copies? You put the paper in the machine, close the cover, and press print. Paper. Cover. Button. Repeat. That's all."

"It's not as simple as that, sir."

"They have a special copier class in law school?"

"No, but I'm sure we can—"

"And what the hell does this mean?" He shoved the bill in Percy's face.

"I don't know, sir. I'm sure I could get Mr. Bacon and he can—"

"Fuck Bacon, fuck this bill, and fuck you. I'm not paying."

"But we just won you a thirteen-million-dollar lawsuit."

Lemonjelo slapped Percy's face with the bill.

Percy had experience dealing with hotheads. He knew a little TLC and coffee went a long way.

"Don't be like that. Why don't we sit down, have a cup of coffee, and relax?"

Percy turned to the coffee maker and poured a cup while singing *We Can Work It Out*, by The Beatles.

Lemonjelo replied with a beatdown. Turned out he'd thought about the bill and didn't feel like hugging out his issues with the firm. Fans of animal mauling would have loved it.

2

PERCY HAD NEVER ENVISIONED working for a firm like Canker Shore. He'd gone to Columbia Law School, but had a hard time getting a job because he didn't interview well. He was a drooler with hands so sweaty they dripped. To make matters worse, the interview period occurred during ragweed season, so the random, intense, mucus-laden sneezing fits didn't bode well for his prospects. He tried allergy shots, but had an allergic reaction to them. The only medication that worked put him to sleep. A drowsy, drooling, sweaty-palmed dweeb did not strike confidence in the heart of any interviewer.

Percy had waited tables during the summer of his second year. Disclosing his law school status hadn't hurt his opportunity as an "over-educated" applicant. It got him employment at every restaurant in town. What high-school dropout wouldn't leap at the chance to lord over a Columbia Law School student?

In his third year, he got a job at Canker Shore LLP because another law student died due to injuries sustained during a case with Dick Bacon. Bacon was the kind of attorney whose cases, if you survived, would end your career at the firm. Anyone staffed on cases with him quit within a month. The managing partner at Canker Shore had submitted the job to Columbia Law's career services on a dare. They were amazed that it had worked. Having a guy from Columbia Law validated the firm.

Even a guy like Percy Winkler.

3

SPRAWLED ON A COT inside an immaculate office, Percy tenderized his swollen, spittooned face with a cool bottle of Cristal labeled "TYSON SETTLEMENT 1992".

Dick Bacon, a white Johnnie Cochrane, didn't notice. Bacon banned his whipping boys from making eye contact with him. He didn't want to see the havoc his legal style wreaked on their faces. As a result, Bacon couldn't pick Percy out of a perp lineup. Couldn't describe his face to a criminal forensic sketch artist. So Bacon didn't see how Percy barely resembled his driver's license photo. Bacon was too busy admiring his reflection in the other settlement trophies. Settlement trophies revealing an unsettled man.

*   *   *

FOR THE UNINITIATED, there couldn't be a more thankless job at big firms than litigation. Litigation clients stewed over these fees even if they won. Corporate clients didn't worry about fees. Their mergers lacked the deep-seated hostility found in litigation matters. Legal fees represented a fraction of what they made in the underlying merger. Like somebody treating you to an extravagant meal so long as you paid the coat check attendant. As a result, corporate clients at the end of deals lavished their attorneys with fantastic and expensive meals and gifts extolling their greatness.

Litigation attorneys received Charlie Brown at Halloween treatment.

They got rocks.

Dick Bacon had none of this. As a litigation partner, he tired of not receiving any of the trophies bestowed upon his corporate peers. Dick Bacon would not debase himself by stewing or begging for such trinkets.

He created his own.

A few years back, he had represented a number of wrestlers involved in the 1991 WWF steroid scandal. Word broke out amongst all juicers that Bacon was the man you'd want representing you. Didn't matter if it was professional athletes, their spouses, gyms, supplement companies or even the Chinese women's swim team.

*　　*　　*

"I HAD ORANJELO just where I wanted…"

Bacon reminisced about events occurring earlier that day when he had interrogated Oranjelo, Lemonjelo's brother and thugged-out Vin Diesel lookalike, who had blubbered with guilt. Bacon nodded at a nervous Percy.

"He had penitence oozing from every orifice."

"Oozing like a yeast infection, sir."

"But that did not stop me, did it, Percy?"

"It never does, sir."

"My penetrating probing turned him into a raging volcano."

"Mount Vesuvius, sir."

"Mount Vesuvius, Percy. And in a last-ditch effort to salvage his wounded pride, he grabbed his mangled pencil. He was ready to pounce on me, like Gladiator Maximus charging Caesar. And what did you do, Percy?"

"I ducked."

"You ducked. Percy, we have a formula for success." He demonstrated his point by gesturing to his numerous self-made legal settlement awards and trophies with the pomp of a Barker girl at the *Price Is Right's Showcase Showdown.*

"I provoke our opponents. They get angry. I rile them some more. They want blood. And you, Percy, give them blood. We settle. Our clients win. Am I clear, Percy?"

Percy nodded.

"When the beast is ready to pounce, do your job and lead with your ear, Percy. Lead with your ear." He pulled his own ear for emphasis.

"Sir, maybe if I—"

"Maybe if you what, Percy? Maybe if you followed directions, I would not have to waste billable time correcting your mistakes? Maybe if you passed the bar, you could practice the law instead of doing glorified paralegal work? Maybe if you tried not to profane everything that is sacred to my profession, you could do something other than walking in here from the gutter and sullying my clients with your stench of malodorous legal naiveté?"

"Maybe I should go to that Bar function now, sir."

"Oh, there's no maybe about that, Percy."

4

FAILING THE BAR four times had rendered Percy unemployable. One employer suggested he stay at Canker until he passed. "After all, somebody must like you there, if they haven't fired you after the second time you failed."

That somebody was Bacon. Canker partnership didn't get in Bacon's way because he brought in the billables and Percy's bar failures made them feel better about themselves. Especially if they had attended shitty law schools.

No public interest organization wanted Percy because his legal experience was too narrow for their needs. He was overqualified for the non-legal corporate positions and underqualified for the legal ones. Even the restaurants that had offered him jobs in law school weren't interested.

Percy tried overcoming the obstacle by leaving his legal education and experience off his resume. It worked well enough to get Percy an interview. He had eventually received new medication for his allergies, so his interviewing skills improved dramatically. When human resources asked what Percy had been doing from college to the present, Percy replied, "I've been traveling the world. Like Matt Damon in *The Bourne Identity*. But without all that running from the government and killing people stuff."

He didn't know geography that well, so his alleged travel itinerary included fictitious comic-book countries like Latveria, home of Fantastic Four nemesis Dr. Doom.

The interviewer inquired about Latveria's location and

Percy replied, "The Banat region, near Symkaria."

"Sym-what?"

Percy's nervousness led him to rattle off other comic book countries, like Wonder Woman's Themyscira, Baron Bedlam's Markovia, and the Black Panther's Wakanda. He figured he could trick the interviewer as long as he refrained from naming obviously fake locations like Narnia or Middle Earth. Percy considered naming the Justice League's Kooey Kooey Kooey, but didn't want to press his luck.

Turned out he didn't have to. Immediately after the interview, human resources contacted Homeland Security, thinking Percy had spent years training in secret terrorist camps. It didn't take Percy long to get over the controversy, but it killed any federal government work opportunities.

Percy couldn't sue Bacon or Canker Shore if he wanted to work elsewhere. After all, who would want to employ a lawyer fresh from suing his previous employer? Percy abhorred the physical abuse he took at Canker, but it was his only legal job. Dick Bacon was the only attorney for whom he worked, so Dick Bacon would be his sole employment reference. He was stuck with a degree that was meaningless and debt that was crippling.

The average person would have filed for bankruptcy, faked their death, or left the country. However, that was not how Percy rolled. Percy Winkler might have been a nebbish. Percy Winkler might have used a nightlight for fear of the Boogeyman, but Percy Winkler was not a quitter. He was in a predicament, but dangumbit, Percy Winkler was going to be a man. A girly man, but a man nonetheless. A man who overcame his problems with dignity. Passing the bar exam would be Percy's first step towards emancipation.

5

THE NEXT DAY, PERCY found Bacon picking his nose with a pyramid-shaped trophy while barking instructions on the phone.

"I don't care if he's on life support, we can still bill."

Bacon ended the call by throwing the phone halfway across the room. It shattered upon hitting the wall. That was the third phone he had destroyed that week.

"Percy, I've been waiting for you. That's time that could've been billed."

Percy crumpled, shoulders hunched, silent.

"Don't just stand there. We have to go to the hospital." He bolted past Percy. "Chop, chop, Percy."

As the two rushed out of the office, Bacon gestured to his manservant Wentworth, perched with Bacon's coat and hat at the ready.

Wentworth drove Bacon and Percy to Bellevue hospital. Upon arriving, Bacon barreled through the hospital and marched into a room that housed a comatose man on life support. Wentworth shuffled three steps behind.

Percy huffed, barely keeping up.

"What are we doing here, sir?"

"He's about to go into surgery."

"He's a client?"

"A lawyer. He has to Bates stamp. Wentworth?"

Wentworth pulled out a stack of papers and a stamp.

"Mr. Bacon, I don't get it."

"Tell him, Wentworth."

"In litigation, all documents need to be stamped with a number. It's called Bates stamping."

"I still don't get it."

"Stimson is going to do some stamping."

"But he's in no condition to—"

Bacon opened Stimson's stiff hand, finger by finger, and positioned a rubber stamp in Stimson's limp hand before clutching it shut. Wentworth placed paper underneath the stamp as Bacon forced Stimson's hand to stamp the paper.

"Wentworth, when are the rest of the documents coming?"

"In a few minutes, sir."

"Great. Surgery isn't for another three hours."

The stamping continued until doctors entered in full surgical gear, sneering, pacing, staring at the clock.

"That's enough, Mr. Bacon."

Bacon nodded curtly. "Just one more."

Nurses descended on Bacon, Percy, and Wentworth and placed them in gowns.

Bacon convened a small conference with Percy and Wentworth a few feet away.

"Wentworth, we're billing this. Two partners, one first-year associate and a paralegal."

"Yes, sir."

Percy scanned the room. Eyes narrowed. Eyebrows squished together.

"Where's the other partner?"

Bacon pointed to a still comatose Stimson.

"Mr. Bacon, how can we bill the client for Stimson?"

"He's here, isn't he?"

"Yes."

"Do you see that heart monitor beeping?"

"Yes."

"That means he's here. Therefore we bill."

"But he's not doing anything."

"Canker Shore is a service firm. We are paid by billing. If

you're working on a case for the client, you're billing. If you're on the subway and you think about a case, you're billing."

"Stimson is unconscious, sir."

"Do you know what he's dreaming of?"

"No."

"Well, I do. He's thinking about the case, so he's billing. As long as that thing beeps he's—"

The monitor flatlined and Bacon flipped out.

"Resuscitate him!"

The doctors tried everything, twice, but nothing worked.

"Try again. Wentworth, we're still billing!"

Stimson was still toast.

"Again! Try again!"

"Sir, he's dead."

"Wentworth," Bacon raved, "we're still billing. Doctor, bring that man back!"

"I'm sorry, but we can't. He's dead."

Hospital staff placed Stimson on a gurney before rolling him down the hallway. Bacon, Wentworth, and Percy sprinted behind them.

"Wentworth, we're still billing!"

"Yes, sir."

"Doctor, can you check his pulse?"

"How many times do I have to tell you? He's dead."

"Are you sure? For all we know, he could have one of those post-life thingies."

"Not likely."

"Wentworth, we're still billing."

"Yes, sir."

Percy couldn't contain his shittiness any longer.

"Maybe we can have a séance, so we can still bill."

"That's a good idea. A really good idea! Wentworth, get me a psychic. We're still billing. Percy, you have a future at Canker Shore."

* * *

LATER THAT NIGHT, Percy walked by Bacon's

office. It reeked of Jim Bean.

"Sir?"

"Come in, Percy."

Bacon slumped in the chair, saggy, arms hanging at his sides. "I can't believe it. Stimson's dead."

"Sorry, sir."

"I worked with that man since I was a summer associate. He ate, slept, breathed, and lived Canker. You could have learned a lot from him, Percy."

"I'm sure I could have, sir."

"The mind of that man? Incredible. His resourcefulness? Godly. Our firm will deeply miss him. And I will too."

"A real shame, sir."

"Do you have any idea long he practiced law? Fifty years. Fifty years of hard work is gone forevermore. Not only that, a father is gone. A husband is no more. How in the world can you replace a man like that?"

"I'm sure that with hard work, Canker can recover."

"Our firm will not recover for decades. Do you have any idea how much he was worth? Seven hundred and fifty dollars an hour. That's how much. Oh well. Just means we'll have to work more hours just to make ends meet. Before you go home, young Percy, to the last full night of sleep we can afford, I need you to meet with Cephus and discuss the Dallas Deal."

6

THE "DALLAS DEAL", code for "bullshit lawsuit", involved a copyright infringement case rejected by every firm in town but Canker Shore. The client, Cephus Billingsly, had seemed normal enough when Percy and Bacon first met with him. Until he asked to check the room for bugs.

Bacon assured him that Canker Shore did not allow vermin to run rampant within its hallowed walls.

Cephus wasn't referring to insects. He feared electronic surveillance devices embedded in the walls by the government. Cephus claimed to have engineered a master plan for catching the DC sniper. Instead of paying Cephus the reward, the feds had allegedly sneaked into Cephus' apartment and found his plans for a rail system running along the East Coast. The feds had pilfered the plans and sold them to Tom Hanks, who had turned them into a movie known as *The Polar Express*.

Percy said, "Mr. Billingsly, *The Polar Express* was based on a book."

"Then this conspiracy is even deeper than I expected. We need to sue the publishers, too."

Percy bit his hands to contain his laughter. Bacon kept a straight face and did the rest of the talking, making the meeting even more hilarious. As soon as Cephus left the office, Percy started cracking jokes.

"Sir, did you hear that? The rail system running along the East Coast he allegedly created already exists. It's called

Amtrak. Maybe we can sue them, too."

Bacon's eyes lit up. "Percy, you have your moments."

Percy wrongfully interpreted that to mean 'moments of comedy'.

"That's why, Percy, I'm giving Cephus to you."

"Excuse me, sir?"

"Clients like Cephus come once in a lifetime."

"He's crazy, sir."

"Are you qualified to make psychological evaluations, Percy?"

"No, sir. But you don't need to be Dr. Phil to know that guy has some serious issues."

"Eccentric, Percy, is the term I believe is more appropriate."

"Because he's rich?"

"That's right, Percy. He can afford to be strange. Which means he can afford our services unless the court deems him mentally unfit."

"How do we know he doesn't already have that designation?"

"He pays a retainer of fifty thousand dollars before we start working on his case. If the check clears, he's competent enough for Canker Shore and our assistance."

"He's not playing with a full deck, sir."

"Name one client who is playing with a full deck, Percy."

Percy couldn't.

"You have the unmitigated gall to question that man's desire to have justice, Percy? You suggest we enact legislation restricting eccentric people from retaining attorneys? Maybe they should sip at different drinking receptacles, so they don't sully your precious water fountains. Or better yet, why don't we just round them up and put them on trains, Percy. Would that make you happy?"

It wouldn't. Neither would bleeding Cephus dry. Cephus reminded Percy of Corky from *Life Goes On*.

As a compromise, Percy quietly kept the costs low by avoiding hourly researching charges on Westlaw and Lexis by using books in Canker's library, minimizing interaction with Cephus so as not to ratchet billable fees for client communication, and avoiding conference calls with Bacon which would have resulted in an additional six-hundred-and-fifty-dollar-per-hour fee.

Bacon found out and needed additional measures to make that money honey, so asked Lance to supervise Percy on the case.

Lance's ascent once again proved the adage 'the cream rises to the top' wasn't always true. Sometimes, scum rises too, and not just to the top of a dirty pool or on *Survivor*. Lance's immunity idol happened to be Yale Law School. It had a transformative effect with Percy feeling like SpongeBob SquarePants, Canker as Bikini Bottom, Cephus as Patrick, and Lance as Sheldon J. Plankton.

In the SpongeBob universe, Plankton lorded his education over everyone else to no avail. At Canker Shore, it made a world of difference. All Lance had to do to pull an E.F. Hutton was mention Yale Law, and everyone listened. Percy didn't appreciate how deep he was by referencing the Plankton analogy, because Percy wasn't down with science like that.

If he were down with science like that, Percy would've known planktons were parasitic crustacean copepods that fed off sharks. At Canker, clients were the sharks' prey and partners were the sharks from which Lance planktoniously leeched his meals. Like plankton, Lance let partners/sharks do all the work. He never took copyright, didn't bother doing any research on Cephus' case, and never worked with Bacon. It was the same with other cases, but it didn't matter. The partners didn't want Lance for his legal insight, the partners needed Lance to sit in on client meetings because it validated them. Yale Law served as protective coating, much like the copepod's exoskeletal armor. Lance could come and go as he pleased, dressed however he liked. That kind of power could've led to numerous fashion faux-pas, but Lance was old-school. A standard grey jacket and slacks did the job.

Percy knew Cephus' case would be rejected the first time their opponents filed a Motion to Dismiss. He suggested dropping the case, because according to court trends, the Southern District wouldn't have any grounds for supporting their position. Lance didn't cower.

Lance made some shit up.

Lance suggested that dicta in the Eastern District added credence to Cephus' crazed claim. He referenced nonexistent cases involving the rule against perpetuities, latches, and the peppercorn theory, which were typical gobbledegook terms lawyers employed to dazzle and confuse layfolks.

Percy wasn't a layperson. He knew that none of the legal concepts had anything to do with the case. He didn't want to embarrass Lance on the spot, because it would have reflected poorly on the firm. Percy knew dicta was mere suggestion instead of an established holding, that the dicta Lance referenced didn't exist, and that not one motion had passed muster under Judge Sanders citing dicta, but Percy played along with his own chicanery.

"Lance, that may be true for the matters in the districts of Latveria, Themyscira, Markovia, and Kooey Kooey Kooey, but in the Eastern District, Judge Sanders is notorious for dismissing dicta as non-persuasive. Cephus, just drop the case."

"But Tom Hanks took my idea."

"Cephus, there are three thing you need to learn about your case. First, you have no case. Second, ideas aren't copyrightable. Third, Tom Hanks always wins. End of story."

It was the first time anyone had spoken frankly to Cephus about the pointlessness of his case. Attorneys at other firms had rejected Cephus as a client because they claimed conflicts with Tom Hanks. Percy had mustered up the courage to be honest because he wanted to prove to Lance that faced with easy paydays, attorneys could be honorable.

Cephus agreed with Percy. Lance, not wanting to lose this battle and the chance for easy billables, piped in.

"Percy, have you drafted motions like this before? If so,

do you have any on hand?"

"I have, and as a matter of fact, I do."

Percy took out some documents and they flew all over the place. Lance, wearing an expression usually only seen during colonoscopy exams, scanned the papers.

"I don't see your name noted anywhere. Are you sure you drafted these? Cephus, do you see Percy's name anywhere on these motions?"

Cephus may have been delusional, but he could read.

"I don't see it."

Percy winced. "That's because I'm not admitted to the New York Bar." He cleared his throat. "Just a formality. That's all."

Lance smelled blood.

"Oh, I understand. You just haven't filled out the paperwork to get admitted."

"We've been through this before, Lance. I can't apply for admission until I pass the bar."

"And if you haven't passed the bar, then you're not a lawyer, are you?"

The truth hurt. All Percy could do was say something that would be so articulate and brilliant, it would stun Lance into submission.

"Lance, I wrote these motions."

Lance pressed on. "Supervised, I hope. If not we could get sanctioned, Cephus. Unless—"

Cephus leaned in to Lance. "Unless what?"

Lance concocted a convoluted plan with a lot of unnecessary research and analysis including months on Westlaw, trips to Hollywood and the Library of Congress, retaining literary experts to analyze the relationship between *The Polar Express* movie and book, structural evaluations of Amtrak juxtaposed with Cephus' rail plans, and acquiring additional staff and paralegals under Lance's wing. "This case demands we turn over every stone, exhaust every conceivable possibility, before we know, with certainty, the merits of your case. The road will be long and it will be costly, but did not

Nelson Mandela say 'Life is worth far much more than gold could ever be'?"

Actually, Bob Marley had sung that in *Jamming* on his *Exodus* album, which made sense since, unbeknownst to Cephus, Lance saw this as prime opportunity for a paid exodus to jam it with some cuties on the beaches of Montego Bay.

Lance ended his Ponzi legal scheme by aping Caveman Lawyer.

"But what would I know? I'm just a graduate of Yale Law School. I don't understand crass, capitalistic, ambulance-chasing concepts like 'billable hours' or 'attorneys' fees'. But I do know this: If you kill this case, you are killing everything that is sacred about our justice system. And you're letting Tom Hanks, and his insipid brand of evil... win."

Cephus pounded the table, shot up from his chair, and extended a hand to Lance. "I like the way you think, mister."

Lance didn't care for physical contact with the humanoids. Instead of a handshake, Lance handed his business card to Cephus.

Percy didn't want Cephus to leave without his info, so he tore a sheet from a legal pad and wrote his name and number on it.

"I'd give you a card, but I'm not admitted yet. But a number's a number, right?"

Percy might as well have given Cephus a used snot rag. Cephus left the info on the table and gave Percy the strangest handshake. Ever.

Lance escorted Cephus away, but poked his head back in the room and pointed to Percy's information. "Percy, could you pick up your trash before you leave? This is a green firm after all." Lance left humming *Jamming*.

7

IF YOU AREN'T an attorney, you haven't seen the City Bar Association's grand interior, adorned with mothballs, old flesh, and marble. Lots of marble. Security wouldn't let you in. But let's say it did. You'd find a strange mix of an old-school firm, a court building and a nursing home. You wouldn't be allowed upstairs. But if you were, portraits of old, crotchety white men and a painting of Supreme Court Justice Ruth Bader Ginsburg would greet you.

Ginsburg seemed to be the female portrait of choice amongst stuffy white legal institutions. At Columbia Law School, there was quite a ruckus involving her portrait. Not only did it not look like her, it was the only portrait hanging near the law-school cafeteria. It made one wonder if her culinary might was as legendary as her legal jurisprudence. Her placement near the cafeteria almost matched the surreal placement of African-American cultural icon (and Columbia Law alum) Paul Robeson's bust near the bathroom wearing a look of joyous post-dump relief.

Percy felt demoted, but that wasn't the reason why he was at the Bar. He was there to represent Canker at a young associates' event. He hadn't been planning to attend, but his best friend and James Bond alternate Rufus Wang had talked him into campaigning for it.

"It will raise your visibility, Percy. The firm will stand behind you."

Canker didn't feel Percy was an appropriate representative.

After an active begging campaign—coupled with a few tears—the firm relented.

At the event, lawyers wearing nametags with the suffix "ESQ." packed the second floor. Percy checked in with Rufus.

Throughout law school, he and Percy had indulged in nerdy delights. Watching Japanese wrestling. Attending comic book conventions. Fan expos.

Problem was? No women. The turning point had come at a post-convention party at a hotspot named Limelight. Percy had paced outside of the converted church nightclub. Rufus, wearing glasses, shit-faced drunk, fucked with the velvet rope. A cock-diesel bouncer gestured for him to stop. Rufus still fucked with the rope by methodically disconnecting and reconnecting it.

"Kill that shit."

Rufus dropped the rope and staggered to Percy while the bouncer reconnected the rope.

"Percy. We need to change our game. I'm trying. See?" He yanked up his pants, proudly modeling taupe socks.

"Keep trying with that, Rufus."

"Don't knock it, motherfucker, don't knock it. I'm your role model." He sang the *Be Like Mike* jingle, replacing 'Mike' with 'Rufus'. He staggered toward the rope. Disconnected it again.

The bouncer spoke through his teeth, straining to restrain himself. "Watch it."

Rufus shuffled backwards. "Okay, dude. Chillax."

The bouncer reconnected the rope and openly stared at Rufus as he walked away. As soon as the bouncer turned his back, Rufus ran to the rope, disconnected it, and then bolted. "C'mon, Percy."

The bouncer turned, laid eyes on the disconnected rope, and gave chase. Until Rufus slipped on a pile of dog shit and crashed into a mailbox.

The bouncer? He bounced.

Percy stared, helpless, wanting to help, not wanting to

touch the dog crap. Rufus staggered up, glasses shattered, teeth chipped.

Percy said, "Some fucking role model."

It was the motivation Rufus needed to transition from cartoon to coochie, incorporating dance games into his Playstation rotation, researching the art of seduction, frequenting dance clubs. Percy came along, but didn't devote the time needed to form the chrysalis. Change. Abandon the virgin cocoon.

Rufus disapproved, but never abandoned Percy. Never gave up on their friendship and the pursuit of pimptitude.

Rufus became so tight in his game, he pulled honeys without telling them he was a lawyer. He was against the grain.

You could tell by Becky's lip-licking lingering look soon as Rufus strutted to her registration table. She was not alone. As soon as Rufus set foot in the room, females were all on his knob. Trembling. Moistening. Stroking arms, hair, glass stems.

Rufus grinned. "Duty calls."

Rufus plucked his nametag from a breathless Becky as he was dragged away. Although he got around, the only thing infectious about Rufus was his magnetism. Rufus's inner nerd, a full lap ahead of the competition, handed the baton to Percy's inner nerd. Rufus laid the foundation for Percy to win this race. Percy channeled Rufus, swaggering to Becky.

"Save some for me, big guy. The Wanger and me go way back. Yep, he's learned well."

Becky sneered. "Your name?"

Percy's inner nerd dropped the baton. Percy squeaked, "percy winkler."

Becky scoured the table for his nametag. "I don't see your nametag here."

"I registered five months ago." Actually, Percy had asked Canker to register him five months ago. He wasn't aware that the firm hadn't wanted to pay the eighty-five-dollar registration fee. Becky wasn't aware either, but that didn't mean she was surprised.

*   *   *

BEFORE WORKING IN the Bar's development office, Becky had served as development coordinator for the Bronx Zoo. Becky had raised money by organizing events displaying the deadliest beasts known to man. Insurance premiums as well as fears of animals killing multi-million-dollar donors had run high after Steve Irwin's death. Becky couldn't take the stress and she'd enjoyed *L.A. Law* back in the day, so she'd jumped at the chance to plan events for the New York City Bar.

It didn't take long for Becky to realize that low insurance premiums for attorney events didn't reflect the dangers faced by organizing them.

Attorneys threw fits that would shame a Cambodian Temple Monkey. Attorneys were more venomous than poison dart frogs or Asian cobras. Organizing a herd of Horned Cape Buffalos had proved less stressful than a gaggle of lawyers. Toddler birthday parties at the Monkey House had reduced good behavior expectations. Toddlers could barely wipe their butts, much less read or write. Attorneys, on the other hand, had nineteen years of education and who knew how many years of butt-wiping experience?

For all the hype about their intelligence, attorneys seemed incapable of accomplishing mundane tasks like filling in their name on a form or being able to discern the time an event started from a registration flyer. Plus, attorneys were cheaper than hobos. Trying to nickel-and-dime every chance they could get. Threatening to sue.

Becky's predecessor at the City Bar had lasted halfway into an event. Not because she'd quit. An attorney had complained about his inability to partake in the event because his firm had allegedly forgotten to process a registration payment in a timely manner. The lesson resulting from her firing was simple: Let the attorney win. The same rules didn't apply to non-attorneys attending events unless they were a spouse or client.

*   *   *

WHEN BECKY DIDN'T have any proof of Percy's registration, she knew the drill.

She smiled. Apologized. "I'm sorry, sir." Fixed the error.

"Where do you work?"

"Canker."

Her toes curled. She'd heard of Canker's cheapness and knew they wouldn't pay shit, but kept that to herself and smiled. She took out a pen, created a nametag reading 'PERCY WINKLER, ESQ.', and handed it to him.

"Let me fix that." He crossed out the 'ESQ.'

"What are you doing?"

"I'm not a lawyer."

Becky whipped out a walkie-talkie.

"Mel, we have a situation at reception."

"A situation?" Percy didn't want a situation. Nor did he want to find out who the hell Mel was. Or what Mel did when called to solve situations for Becky. Percy needed action. He took short, shallow breaths.

"Rufus." He channeled Rufus, smirking, leaning forward, oh so suggestively.

"I'm not a lawyer. Technically speaking. But why be technical?"

"This event is for attorneys only. That's what I've been told."

Still filled with the spirit of Rufus, he caressed her hand.

"I'd like to tell you something. You're—"

She blew a rape whistle, sending shockwaves throughout the event:

A nerd held his nerdette tight as a fat fuck tried to hide behind a beanpole gal.

A domestic violence attorney carefully reached for mace.

A sleazeball snatched a spiked drink from a bombshell, guzzled it and the roofie he dropped in earlier.

Security arrived. Not your run-of-the-mill, fat cop rejects. These thick-necked heathens were straight-up goons, warming up their batons by smacking them against walls, tables, and passers-by. Becky jabbed at Percy.

"It's him!"

Percy bounced on his toes. His gestures turned to Jazz hands.

"Hold on a minute—"

Security, with years of built-up aggression towards the attorneys who had belittled them, viewed Percy as their personal piñata. They'd savor this moment. They prodded Percy with their batons, like lions pawing a cornered koala.

Percy alternated shrieking with yelping.

"I work at Canker. I graduated from Columbia Law with Rufus Wang." His eyes darted about the room. "Rufus?"

A new guard emerged, Taser in hand, crackling it on and off. Security neither knew nor cared about Percy's blabbering.

Percy rubbed and twisted his hands. Sweat gushed from every pore. He did not want to be tased, bro. "Wait. I'm a lawyer. I know everyone in here. Like that porker cowering behind the beanpole—"

The fat nerd sucked in his gut.

"That guy passed out on the ground." It was the attempted rapist. Roofies kicked in like a motherfucker.

Security didn't want witnesses. The beating would commence in private. They dragged Percy through the clusterfuck.

Until the crowd parted like the Red Sea from the open men's room door.

There stood Rufus. Towering. Arms akimbo. Pants unzipped. Flanked by floozies.

"Release that man and return to your posts."

His zipper shone brighter than Green Lantern's ring. Security hissed and dropped Percy, retreating to their lair.

Becky stood stunned, staring at his zipper, amazed by the power pulsating from within. Longing for Rufus to butter her biscuits would not suffice. She seized the opportunity to make peace.

"I'm so sorry, Mr. Wang. I had no idea they would treat your secretary with such savagery."

"Secretary?" Percy dusted himself off.

"He'll have to check in downstairs."

Rufus' eyes widened. "Downstairs? After all Mr. Winkler has gone through?"

Becky's chin quivered. "You're right. Please follow me." Becky brushed Percy like a prize hound.

Percy moaned. "Thanks."

Becky replied, "It's my pleasure."

Percy said, "I'm thanking Rufus."

"No problem, Percy." Rufus nodded while adjusting his crotch.

"You really laid down the pipe, I mean law, back there, Rufus."

A receptionist arrived with an inkpad, eyes widened, rounded, unblinking. Becky, lips pursing, snatched the pad from her. "Mr. Winkler will get the star treatment."

Becky massaged Percy's fingers in the most awkwardly erotic way while eye-fucking Rufus. She rolled Percy's fingers in the ink and hummed *Unchained Melody* by the Righteous Brothers.

She purred. "Ever see *Ghost?*"

Rufus was too disgusted to reply. Percy realized she was reenacting the scene where Demi Moore and Patrick Swayze copulated with clay. It was not about Percy. Becky gave Rufus a preview of what she could do to him.

Rufus rolled his shoulders. Focused on the Ginsberg painting for guidance.

Ruth did not approve.

*   *   *

"SO," PERCY ASKED Rufus, "what happened with the consultation in the bathroom?"

Rufus marveled at Percy's ink-caked hands and splattered visitor badge. "Attorney-client privilege."

A voice from the trailer park emerged.

"Attorney-client privilege? Sheeit, ancient Chinese secret."

It was Zeke Thurman, a dapper country boy, offering Rufus an unwelcome and unreturned high-five.

Zeke was far from what you would expect from a New York lawyer. He loved the way things were done in South Carolina and would be damned if New York would make him sissified. He never walked anywhere. He drove. Even if he needed to cross the street, he would get into his car, double-park, and handle his business.

Zeke fancied himself a man of God who sampled sin to understand the trials and tribulations of the common man. It made no sense to Percy. Zeke didn't just sample sin; like an all-you-can-eat buffet, he'd go back for seconds and thirds. Sometimes he'd sneak a doggy bag in case he wanted a snack later.

"When did you get here, Zeke?"

"Nice of you to ask. I don't know why the wife insisted on comin'. I had a hell of a time findin' parkin'."

His wife was one of Rufus's earlier groupies. She slinked up to Zeke. He planted an open-mouthed kiss on her—and nearly tossed his cookies.

"Goddamn, woman. You been eatin' that salty-ass caviar, haven't you? And that little taste is all you saved fo' Big Daddy?"

Percy giggled. He knew the taste came from Rufus's private stock, but not from personal experience. Percy Winkler had played recorder in school, not skin flute.

"There's more where that came from, big guy."

Rufus elbowed him in the ribs. Zeke's wife grabbed and gargled a glass of cabernet. Swallowed. Mouthed 'call me' to Rufus behind Zeke's back.

"Enough with the jibber-jabber." Zeke cackled, "Gimme some of that yellow love, Wanger." He hugged a rigid Rufus. Percy extended a high-five. Zeke opted to shake his hand. In the process, Zeke unwittingly smeared himself with a ginormous gob of ink from Percy's fingerprint molestation massage.

"Hot damn, this place is usually colder than a witch's titty. But today? I'm a roastin' like a Sunday sausage."

Zeke wiped his brow, unknowingly smudging his face with

ink.

"Hey boy, hold this for a second." Zeke dumped his coat on Percy to slap on a nametag which read 'ZEKE THURMAN, ESQ.; NAACP LEGAL DEFENSE FUND'. Percy's face sagged. His chest hitched.

Zeke chuckled. "Now that's what I call some A-ffirmative action. A white boy playin' Kay-toe."

Percy's geek pedigree made him totally aware of the reference. Kato, or Kay-toe, as Zeke called him, was an Asian manservant to white superhero Green Hornet. Nobody else got the joke, but that didn't stop other attorneys from treating Percy like a bellhop, piling coats in his arms. Cheap-ass bastards didn't even tip.

"The Emancipation Proclamation was a long time ago, boy." Zeke chortled. "You is free now, ya heah?"

Percy tried winning back some cool points. "Sorry to bust your bubble, Bubba. But I is free. I mean, I am free."

A bandaged lackey piled more coats in Percy's coat-laden arms.

Zeke, still sweltering, spread so much ink over his face he looked like a blackface minstrel.

"Say, I never caught your name, boy."

"You don't remember Contracts class? You, me, and Rufus?"

Zeke seized a handful of chicken wings from a floating waiter and stuffed his Jolsonfied face.

"That's right. You that fella with the dong, starrin' in them skin flicks after law school."

"Nope. Although it's not the first time I've been confused for a porn star. Right, Rufus?"

"Sure, Percy."

As a black lawyer pitched his coat at Percy, Zeke extended his hand and flashed a bright smile.

Percy wasn't finished. "All cocksmithery talk aside, I—"

A photographer asked Rufus for a photo and he responded by posing with Percy. Percy put his arm around the black lawyer. Before the photographer took the photo,

Zeke shoved Percy out of the way and hugged the black attorney and Rufus for a prime photo op.

Instead of cheese, Zeke shouted Kumbaya.

8

THE NEXT DAY at Canker, Percy deposed T-Bone, a thug layered with muscles, in a fishbowl at Canker Shore.

T-Bone squinted as the sun shone in his eyes. Bacon nodded at Percy as T-Bone's lawyer, Irwin, cleaned his glasses with tremendous frustration.

T-Bone couldn't take it anymore.

"For the love of God. Could you please close the shade? I'm going blind over here."

Bacon sneered to Percy, who fiddled with the window shade. His efforts bombarded T-Bone with sunlight.

T-Bone was livid and Percy felt guilty, but Bacon gestured for him to leave the shade alone and continue questioning.

"Okay. Mr. T-Bone, this—"

"Penile implant."

Percy was beyond embarrassed. "Yes, that thing. You stated earlier that our doctors said it was safe?"

"Are you deaf?"

"I'm sorry, but I have to ask."

"What the fuck you think?"

Bacon scribbled on a note card before handing it to Percy.

"Um, are you sure that it wasn't caused by—"

Percy flashed uncertainty but didn't want to upset Bacon.

"Are you sure that, that you're sure that, it wasn't caused by excessive masturbation resulting from excessive steroid-induced shrinkage which is a byproduct of your latent homosexuality?"

T-Bone pounced on Percy.

Bacon was pleased.

Irwin struggled to stop T-Bone before bolting the room.

"We need security, now!"

9

PERCY NEEDED A few bottles of Bacon's celebratory Cristal to dull the aches.

"Percy, the bar is coming up." Every time Bacon used Percy's name, it sounded like he was saying 'Pussy' instead.

"I know that, sir."

"We cannot bill you as an attorney if you do not pass, Percy."

"I know, and I appreciate the firm's bearing with me."

"This is your last chance, Percy."

"I know, sir, and appreciate the time off."

"Time off, Percy? I need you here."

"Sir, you approved my leave months ago. I have the tickets—"

"Doesn't matter."

"I purchased the hotel room."

"Doesn't matter."

"It's non-refundable."

Bacon played the world's smallest violin.

Percy said, "But how am I going to study?"

"I am sure if you plan your time wisely, Percy, you will be able to find the time."

"When I'm working nineteen-hour days, including weekends?"

"I am sure you will figure it out, you Percy."

"Excuse me, sir?"

"What?"

"You said 'you Percy'."

"Never mind what I said, just go."

10

"YOU'RE STILL GOING, PERCY."

Percy looked at Rufus askance. "What you talkin' 'bout, Rufus?"

"I knew Bacon would pull some shit. So I handled it."

"Handled what?"

"You go on your study trip to Geneva as planned."

"What about Bacon?"

"I got this, Percy. Trust me." His smile unnerved Percy.

"Rufus—"

"I got this." Rufus gave Percy an unwelcome shoulder rub. "All will be well. Trust me, Dusty."

"Dusty?"

"JYD, Hulkster, whatever you prefer."

"You're freaking me the fuck out, Rufus."

"Look, just go to Geneva. Don't answer your phone. Just study. And don't come back to town until it's bar time, got it?"

Before Percy could respond, Rufus pulled him out of his seat. "C'mon, Percy. Move it."

Percy shrugged him off. "I'm freshly injured, man."

"Percy, go to Geneva. Stay in Geneva. Don't answer your phone. Don't come back to Manhattan until it's time to take the bar, got it?"

Percy didn't. But what choice did he have? Bacon had broken his word. After breaking Percy's face. Repeatedly.

Little did he know what Rufus meant by 'handling it.'

Good thing he didn't.

BACON COULDN'T BELIEVE HIS EYES.

"Let me get this straight, Percy. Last night, you were in a car accident resulting in emergency cosmetic surgery which requires you to wear a face mask?"

'Percy' was a perfect body double. It was as if he were Percy's long-lost twin. He wore an opaque facemask that distorted his features. Whoever Rufus had hired had a knack for finding stunt-double stand-ins with Hollywood-type accuracy.

Not that it mattered.

Bacon had banned Percy from making eye contact with him. Bacon didn't want to see the havoc his legal style wreaked on Percy's face. As a result, Bacon couldn't pick Percy out of a perp lineup. Couldn't describe his face to a criminal forensic sketch artist. So Bacon wouldn't know how closely Percy's stand-in resembled Percy.

Bacon had no choice but to suspend his disbelief, since he had never known anyone who had survived a devastating car accident.

"And you're still taking the bar next week?"

"I'm passing the bar next week."

"Really?"

"One hundred percent guaranteed, Mr. Chitterlings."

"Excuse me?"

"That's not your name?"

"My name is Bacon, Percy."

"That's right. Sorry, sir."

"The accident must have jarred your brain, Percy."

"Jarred my brain."

"No need to worry. We can still bill you out. As a matter of fact, I'd assume that you were thinking about work all during your hospital stay, correct, Percy?"

"Yes, sir, Mr. Bacon."

"Then we have nothing to worry about. Carry on."

*   *   *

THE IMPOSTER REALIZED his goof while he was inside the bathroom. His crib notes read "CHITTERLINGS = BOSS".

"Fuckin' mamalukes."

He replaced "CHITTERLINGS" with "BACON".

He took advantage of the free mouthwash dispensed in every bathroom at Canker, courtesy of a partner who blamed an associate's bad breath for losing a case.

*   *   *

LATER THAT DAY, while the Imposter yakked on the phone, Bacon's secretary Sandy noticed Lance spying on him.

"What's the matter?"

"Something's different about him."

"I think it's a new tie."

"He's acting funny."

"He just had cosmetic surgery."

Lance couldn't give it a rest. Throughout the day, he stalked the Percy Imposter from afar as the Imposter typed on the computer, rifled through law books, and met with Bacon.

As the Imposter left the office, Lance followed, eventually yelling "Winkler!"

The Imposter ignored him and Lance chased after him.

The Imposter darted through traffic, unable to shake Lance.

"Stop!"

The Imposter didn't.

Neither did a dump truck, which crushed the poor

Imposter. Before a crowd could gather, Lance skulked away.

12

THE REAL PERCY STUDIED in Geneva, located in the Finger Lakes region of Upstate New York. Percy knew the Bar prep lectures weren't worth attending in person, so he ordered the DVDs and viewed the trip as a study retreat.

He refrained from sampling Geneva's famous winemaking so he could focus on his tight schedule. His practice test results sucked, but Percy knew the actual exam was the only thing that mattered.

He enjoyed the quiet region as a study haven, but didn't think the sleepy town was anywhere he'd choose to live until he was a grandpa. Not to suggest Percy had kids. To his knowledge, he didn't. Still, Percy knew he'd be back to take advantage of the hooch, and if he passed the bar, his abstinence would be worth it.

In between study sessions, Percy remembered his third bar exam failure. At the time, Bacon had sent him on a document review in Westchester County. Percy still had a test scheduled for Manhattan. He'd perfectly planned a timely arrival: early departure from his hotel with a car service to the Amtrak station and an early train to NYC.

A half-hour after leaving the station, Percy's train crashed into a herd of cows. Percy couldn't believe it and feared going through another round of studying. He leapt from his seat.

"No, no, no!" he yelled.

The conductor rushed him and asked if Percy was fine.

"Yes, I mean, no. We have to start the train."

"We can't do anything until the police arrive."

Percy pushed him aside and opened the door.

"What are you doing, sir?"

Percy started to jump off the train, but the conductor grabbed him by the collar.

"Sir, have you lost your mind?"

"I have to make it to New York."

"You're in New York."

"I know this is New York, but it isn't New York."

"What other New York is there?"

"The one with skyscrapers, the Statue of Liberty and my goddamn test."

The conductor yelled out for assistance. Percy grew more frantic.

"What the hell are you doing?"

"We need you to calm down, son. You might have suffered a concussion."

"I'm fine."

"But you said you didn't know where you were."

"I do know where I am, and that's the problem."

"That's for the doctor to decide."

"Are you mad?"

Additional conductors and the food car worker, who was in the middle of mixing nacho sauce, pounced on Percy and held him down. Nacho sauce from the worker's hands dripped into Percy's nose and almost drowned him. Gasping for air, Percy moaned, "I have a test. Let me go, I have a test."

The workers thought Percy was crazy.

Percy eventually made it to Manhattan, but he was five hours late, so the bar administrators wouldn't let him in. He asked the bar association for an opportunity to take the test that week, but was told he had to wait until winter. To make matters worse, the smell of nacho sauce haunted his sensory memory for days. Percy detected it everywhere, even above the presence of real pungent odors. Percy tried every air freshener known to man. Without success.

Percy's problem was so bad it affected his eating habits. The smell contaminated every item on his plate. He'd return his food orders, claiming they were spiked with nacho cheese.

Rufus had had enough, so he took Percy to Harlem and tried every incense vendor within a ten-block area. Within two blocks, they'd already met with about twenty incense salesmen. Each one lit a number of sticks to remedy Percy's nasal hauntings. But to no avail. Defeated, Percy and Rufus got into a cab and headed back to midtown. Suddenly, Rufus spied a black guy dressed like a genie and stopped the cab. He had a feeling about the guy. Percy had a feeling too… that the guy looked like Mr. Popo from *Dragonball* Z. Rufus walked over to the incense vendor and explained the problem. Mr. Popo reached into a bag and pulled out an incense stick he waved like a magic wand.

Percy asked, "What's it called?"

"Pussy."

"Figuratively speaking, right?"

"Nope. It smells like pussy."

Rufus nabbed it from Mr. Popo, took a whiff, and said, "This doesn't smell like any pussy I've had."

Popo replied, "Then maybe you need to rethink the pussy you've been getting."

The comeback hooked Percy, but Rufus wanted to light the incense and test its effectiveness before purchasing.

Popo refused.

"You want me to get arrested? You can't air pussy out in public."

Percy paid for the sticks and took them home. Pussy lifted Percy's nasal curse within seconds. He marveled at its power and returned to the corner to find Popo. Alas, he wasn't on the corner.

He was across the street.

Percy didn't notice, which made his version of the story more interesting than the truth.

13

AT CANKER, LANCE TOWERED over Sandy, who was cleaning out Percy's office.

"I can't believe it."

There was a bizarre, new sensation rippling through Lance. Guilt.

"He had the worst luck in the world."

"To die like that."

"Bad Luck Schleprock."

Suddenly, a husky voice bellowed.

"Who the fuck died and pissed in your Cocoa Puffs this morning?"

It was a masked, muscle-bound goon wearing a neck-brace, in the doorway.

"Can I help you, sir?"

The goon hunched his posture and slightly weaved.

"You don't recognize me, Sandy? It's me. Percy."

Lance blinked rapidly. "I thought the truck smote you."

"The doctors, God bless 'em, they saved my life."

Lance gaped, stuttered, his mouth opened and closed. "But you're taller and wider."

"It's the drugs. The techniques they used to save my life changed my body. Kinda like the Incredible Hulk. Or Bane, if you prefer DC Comics and Batman. So you don't has to worry none. I'm back and headin' to meet Lemonjelo once I get my ass a shake." He goosed Sandy on his way out.

Lance glanced around, looking for answers.

"That couldn't be Percy, could it?"

Sandy shrugged half-heartedly. "My sister-in-law was on steroids for her thyroid. She grew a beard."

Lance pursed his lips. "Did she also grow five inches? Muscle mass? A husky voice?"

"Did she ever. My brother actually preferred her that way. You know, her clitoris actually swelled to the size of a—"

"Goodbye, Sandy."

*   *   *

INSIDE A CONFERENCE room, Lemonjelo spat tobacco as soon as he laid eyes upon the milkshake-sucking Percy imposter we'll just call 'Goon'.

"It's about goddamn time you got here."

Goon was unfazed. "Wassup?"

Lemonjelo spoke through clenched teeth. "The New York Bar Association told me to get an itemized bill and guess what I found?" He waved a bill. "Hundreds of overpriced copies per week for eight months."

"No shit? Lemme see." Goon probed the bill. "Fuck. This shit costs a nickel a copy at Slim's."

"What the fuck is Slim's?"

"A place that makes cheaper copies."

"No shit."

"We are most certainly fuckin' you over, my friend."

"So what are you going to do?"

Goon handed the bill back to Lemonjelo. "I'm gonna finish my shake."

As Goon walked away, Lemonjelo's nostrils flared.

"I'll finish you!"

Lemonjelo cleared his sinus cavities to hock the mother of all loogies when Goon stabbed him in the throat with the milkshake straw.

It didn't end there.

Goon beat the living shit out of him. Tobacco juice squirted out of the straw Goon lodged in Lemonjelo's neck.

Goon did what most guys do when pounding an adversary into oblivion. He started talking shit.

"Lemme tell you how this is gonna work. I read your file and it seems as if you ain't payin' enough. Times is tough, so you're gonna help me out."

Lemonjelo gurgled while Sandy leered at the scene with another secretary.

"Must be his medication."

*   *   *

LATER ON, Goon cleaned his teeth with a straw as Bacon inspected a check written by Lemonjelo.

"One hundred dollars a copy?"

"Plus a grand for every hour we work."

"Percy, that's twice our hourly rate."

"That's why I suggested it to him. You know, for all our hard work and shit."

Bacon hugged Goon.

"Getting hit by a truck was the best thing to happen to your career, Percy. Go home and get refreshed. We have a big day ahead of us tomorrow."

As Goon left Bacon's office, Lance entered.

"Mr. Bacon?"

"Lancelot, did you see what Percy did?"

"No offence, sir. But that's not Percy."

"Looks like the same Percy to me."

"Sir, that Percy has grown immensely."

"Did you see Lemonjelo before he was on the juice?"

"No, sir, but—"

"Exactly. Percy had a life-threatening accident. We don't know what kind of experimental steroid treatments they gave that poor Percy."

"I could find out, sir."

"You will do nothing of the sort, Lance."

"But, sir—"

"You will leave Percy alone."

Bacon tossed Lemonjelo's check at Lancelot.

"Lance, when you can turn shit into gold, just like Percy did, we will talk. Until then, Lance, do not waste time that could be far better spent working on billable client matters."

Lance fell mute. Now Bacon used his name like an epithet.

"Take a shower while you're at it, Lance. You absolutely reek with the stench of desperation. And it does not suit you."

14

GENEVA WASN'T SUITING PERCY, either. Everything seemed too new. His hotel room? Immaculate. Just like the way his mother kept things. Every time he looked at the ironed bedsheets or the polished chrome faucet handles, memories of his past failures flooded his mind.

The first time Percy had failed, he had just graduated from law school.

"A loan?" Percy's mother asked.

"Yep. Same guys who give money for living expenses in law school offer loans for the bar."

"They give money for bar study living expenses?"

"Up to two grand."

"That won't be enough."

"I know. That's why I want to stay home to study."

"I don't think you understand. Two thousand dollars is not enough for you to stay at home."

"You're gonna charge me?"

"For room and board? Of course."

Percy blinked rapidly. His parents were cheap, but this was a new low. He didn't have any other living options, so he tried making the most of it. "What if I just pay for my room?"

"It's a package deal. Gourmet chef and all."

"You're bringing in a chef?"

"I am a chef."

"Since when?"

"Since watching Food Network. Plus, you're getting custom meals. Add a mother's love? Priceless."

"How am I supposed to get more money?"

"I'm sure there's work at Starbucks."

"Mom, I'm supposed to be studying for the bar."

"There are twenty-four hours in a day, Percy. You'll have time. Plus, you have chores to do. You don't expect your father to mow the lawn, after all?"

In college, it had taken Percy forty-five minutes to get from his home in Columbia, Maryland to Washington, DC. Percy didn't know things had changed since college. Traffic congestion extended the commute by an hour. Percy considered saving time by taking the DVD course.

"But it's not like a live lecture with question-and-answer sessions," a bar prep rep told him. "You can never discount the value of a live lecture."

Percy believed the hype. It was what kept him sane while caught up in gridlock.

He arrived forty minutes late for his first day of class at the Jefferson Davis University Law School campus. Right in the middle of downtown DC. Searching for parking took almost as long as the DC commute.

After Percy finally found a spot, he rushed to the building, signed in, and was given a security badge.

"Make sure you wear it at all times you're on site," a proctor said.

Percy entered the classroom and did a double-take. There were rows of chairs, peppered with students facing a monitor. He left the room, searched for the proctor and found a new one kicking it to a UPS lady.

Percy smiled. "I think I'm at the wrong place. I'm here for the New York Bar Prep."

The proctor stood upright. "Right. My bad." He winked at the UPS lady and led Percy down the hallway and up two flights of stairs. What Percy heard made him cringe.

Droning. Lecturing. Lawyering.

"Yup. This sounds right."

The proctor whispered, "Keep it down. We don't want to disrupt the lecture."

Percy nodded.

"It's the second door on the right."

Percy flashed a thumbs-up to the proctor and headed towards the lecture. He took a deep breath and tiptoed in.

It was a room smaller than the other. With a televised lecture front and center.

"This can't be right. Maybe it's projected from another room."

Nope.

He noticed a VHS machine under the monitor, with a green play arrow lit.

"A fucking VCR? I'm paying two grand to watch a fucking VHS tape on a fucking VCR?"

A voice in the room replied, "Ain't no fucking on this tape, that's for damn sure."

It was Rufus, alone in the room. Percy took a seat beside him.

Percy sized up the room. "I thought we were paying for a teacher?"

Rufus said, "Maybe he couldn't make it today."

"You're probably right."

He was anything but.

Every day, the proctor played a new tape on different exam subjects. The lecturers varied in style, competency, and teaching ability.

Percy worried about his passing prospects. Rufus couldn't be bothered to care.

"Percy, eighty percent of people who take the New York Bar exam pass the New York Bar exam. It's a test about law school. You went to law school. You graduated from law school. You'll pass."

"But I never learned some of these concepts." Percy thumbed through the course book. "Like fee simple? What the hell is fee simple?" He thrust the book in Rufus's face and tapped the page.

Rufus slapped the book away. "Stop playing."

"Who's playing?" Percy picked up the book and frantically skimmed the pages.

"Didn't you take property?"

"I got an A in it."

"So?"

"So? I took Hawthorne. He spent the entire semester talking about what was wrong with the concept of property. And not once did he say shit about fee simple."

"Guess that means he thought it was fine."

"Rufus."

"Okay. But you got an A in it. That has to count for something."

"I wrote my exam analyzing *Plessy* and *McIntosh*. You know, disenfranchisement of minorities? What I studied at Howard? The son of a bitch thought it was fascinating."

"Whoa, I thought he was your favorite professor? Now he's a son of a bitch?"

"Because I took him for every class you possibly could."

"That means—"

"Yeah, that means I don't know shit about fee simple, felony murder, or conspiracy."

"You had him for Crim Law?"

"And Crim Pro."

"Jesus. You mean—"

"Almost a quarter of the exam subjects."

Rufus inhaled deeply through his nose and exhaled through his mouth. "Percy, we went to Columbia Law School."

"And?"

"And? Do you think they'd entrust classes that important to a meandering fuck-up if it resulted in graduates like you failing the bar?"

Percy thought about it. Hard.

"I'm going to pay for all my law school sins."

"Percy, you're not listening. We went to Columbia Law School, the fourth-ranked law school in the country—"

"Fifth."

"What?"

"Columbia is the fifth-ranked law school in the country. NYU is fourth."

"Whatever. My point is, Columbia Law School is the top-ranked law school in New York and——"

"NYU is the top-ranked law school in New York."

"Goddamn it, Percy. It doesn't matter. Eighty percent of all the motherfuckers who take the New York Bar Exam pass the New York Bar Exam. Only eight percent of applicants get into Columbia Law School, okay? I like your odds."

"What about the grading curve?"

"Ever get a C?"

"No."

"Then I really like your odds."

"At least one of us does."

"Percy, who saved you from wasting time reading cases? Me, that's who. Turned out pretty good, didn't it?"

"It did, but——"

"And you enjoyed law school once you stopped wasting your time in class. In fact, you got better grades, right?"

"Yes."

"Well, I told you what the game was then, and I'm telling you what this bullshit is now. It's the same shit all over again. Only this time, we're taking a test with dumbasses from Fordham and Eggs, Carbozo, and any other homeless shelter posing as a law school. It's more than we did in our third year at Columbia, so we're trying harder. That should count for something, right?"

"I guess."

That was all they had. Guesses. Guesses from silence. Painful silence given their normally big mouths.

Rufus found inspiration. "Let's get a drink after this lecture and see whether DC bars are as wack as they were in college."

"Can't. Have to take my mom to the store."

"Right, have to earn your keep."

"Don't get me started."

Percy was too embarrassed to admit his mother had extorted him to get a job at Starbucks.

Eventually, Percy relented and answered Rufus's call to hang. Considering he served as his mother's chauffeur, gardener, and, yuck, masseuse, Percy was too beat for studying.

And that was what destroyed his chance at passing the New York Bar Exam. He had to teach himself because of bad teaching. Unlike law school, there was no Columbia curve. Making matters worse, he needed to overcome flawed legal conceptions burnished in his brain.

15

GOON HAD NO SUCH BURNISHING while covering for Percy. At a deposition the next day, Bacon toyed with Bruti, a Human Growth Hormone-fuelled slab of meat that bristled with rage. Gladys, bandaged from the last altercation, typed without a care as Bruti's lawyer Larry signaled for a break.

"A minute, Dick."

Bacon took the opportunity to hold a mini-conference with a chuckling Goon.

"Percy, you remember the drill?"

"Baco-bits, this is me. Percyroni is here for you."

"When the beast begins to pounce, you do your duty."

"Got it."

Larry was ready for him to continue and Bacon obliged.

"Bruti, let's pick up where we left off. You attribute your inability to satisfy your wife to performance anxiety?"

Bruti scoffed. "That's what my shrink told me."

"It must have been rough. Suzi is one magnificent creature. Soft skin. Long, luxurious mane. Luscious"—he coughed—"DSLs."

"Excuse me?"

Goon chimed in. "DSLs. Dick-suckin'—"

Bacon finished the sentence. "Lips. I meant lips."

Bruti's lawyer didn't like what he saw.

"Objection. Dick, what does this have to do with anything?"

"Larry, we're talking about divorce on the grounds of abandonment."

"Meanin' no fuckin'," Goon said.

"Suzi is my client," Bacon said, "and I'm just trying to figure out your client's side of the story."

"Dick, we went over this before. I can't stop you from asking these distastefully suspect questions, but be aware that I will present my objections to the Judge."

"Duly noted. May I continue, Bruti?"

"Whatever."

"Great. Now, your wife has D-cup bosoms?"

"Objection. Bruti, don't answer that."

"Larry—"

"Dick, the question's not on point."

"Bruti, Suzi said you couldn't perform your... husbandly duties no matter how hard you tried to compensate for your... sexual inadequacy. You tried penis pumps with ridiculous names ranging from"—Bacon read a list—"'Long Schlong Silver' to 'Bigger Hunga Ding-Dong' to enhance your lack of largesse?"

"Objection. Bruti, you don't have to answer that."

"Bruti, you tried Viagra, but the blood constriction intended to cause erection instead sent you to the emergency room?"

"I had an allergic reaction to it."

"You tried cock rings, cunnilingus, dildos, dolls, strap-ons, swings, Ben Wa balls, beads, leather, lingerie, plugs, pheromones, but to no avail?"

"So what?"

"I'm having a hard time, something you probably aren't familiar with."

"Objection."

"Bruti, given all of your masculine inadequacy, you still don't understand how your wife could consider herself sexually abandoned and therefore desire to seek pleasure elsewhere?"

"No, I don't."

"Well, Bruti, I find your logic as pathetic as you were in bed."

Bruti began to charge Bacon, who expected Goon to step

in. However, Goon stepped to the side, chuckling as Bruti obliterated Bacon.

* * *

BECAUSE OF THE VICIOUS beating inflicted by Bruti, Bacon stayed at the hospital for a few hours. He emerged with a few bone bruises and a neck brace.

He directed all of his frustration at Goon, who hadn't known what he was supposed to do.

"Step the fuck in, Percy! I'm not supposed to look like this. You are!"

"Hey! Calm down. I forgot."

"Are you high, Percy? On my time?"

"It's these goddamn painkillers I gotta take from my accident."

"Painkillers should improve your performance as a punching bag, Percy, not detract from it."

"Next time, I'll write crib notes on my arm. I gots your back."

He slapped Bacon's back, (un)intentionally causing rippling waves of pain across his spine.

16

PAIN RIPPLED ACROSS Percy's brain in Geneva. Failing the bar had trashed his social life. Bar prep courses for the July examination began in May, ruining Percy's summer. There would be no excursions to the Hamptons, Fire Island, Martha's Vineyard, Costa Rica. Prep courses for the February examination began the day after Christmas.

After his first bar failure, Percy decided to celebrate the holidays by going home. His mother looked forward to his arrival and hoped he would stay to study. She wanted to take advantage of his big firm salary.

During Percy's first bar study home, his mother had made a lot of money charging him rent and personal chef fees. When her baby boy failed the bar, she felt terrible. At least until she realized that his firm salary meant he could pay more than his summer student loan.

She planned accordingly by watching *Queer Eye for the Straight Guy*, *Blow Out*, and other self-improvement shows in anticipation of charging Percy for a makeover and daily spa-like treatments. Money received from her last extortion had financed the new flooring, wall décor, furniture and fixtures made of wood and natural stone including granite, marble and soapstone. She modeled her home after a high-end spa, including proper lighting and layout to create a Zen-like atmosphere.

Percy received neither tranquility nor peace once he entered his parents' home and walked right into an argument about a contractor they'd hired to transform their bathroom hallway. He'd done half the job, claiming the contract was for the upper bathroom hallway and not for the lower bathroom hallway.

It was a typical boondoggle.

He refused to do the rest of the hallway without more money. His mother claimed they couldn't sue because of the statute of limitations, a legal concept involving the maximum period of time before legal proceedings based on certain events must be initiated. She didn't know that a number of factors affected the statute's application, because she hadn't gone to law school. Instead of asking Percy, a Columbia alum, she decided to play lawyer her damn self. Percy had been here before and knew he'd get no respect, but tried helping anyway.

He didn't want to rattle off the factors, but when he started to suggest that she needed a legal analysis from an attorney, she cut him off. She considered herself competent enough to do the analysis. She hadn't gone to law school, but felt like it wasn't necessary. She found what she needed on the Internet and had great reading comprehension skills.

Instead of getting help from Percy on her legal problem, she sought assistance from Percy's dad to fetch her purse and take her to the store. After Percy's father left to find the purse, Percy pleaded with his mother to come to him for help with legal issues.

She whispered, "I try to tell your father that, but you know how he is."

"Ma, you were doing it too."

"But you said you didn't want to hear me complain about my problems."

"There's a difference between complaining about the dripping faucet, since I'm not a plumber, complaining about the cable, since I'm not a repairman, and complaining about the law, since I'm a lawyer."

"What about the 'professionals' complaining about relatives and friends asking them professional questions and not wanting to be bothered?"

"The difference is, I'm telling you now, like I've been telling you for years, I am not like those 'professionals.'"

"That's right. Unlike those 'professionals' you haven't passed the bar."

Percy respectfully remained home for Christmas dinner, but left for work the next day. His mother wasn't pleased after all the work she'd done in preparation for his spa treatments. Percy didn't let it bother him because he didn't have room for the anger. His grudge over his extortion during his first exam prep at home took too much space and wasn't budging.

* * *

IN GENEVA, Percy's scores weren't budging. Especially in Criminal Law. No matter how hard he tried, the law wasn't sticking. Percy moved on to another subject, Criminal Procedure, and suffered the same fate. It wasn't until he finally reached Commercial Paper that he found success. It dealt with all aspects of checks: writing, receiving, cashing. He didn't need legal experience to understand it. And it gave Percy a brief respite from his prior failures.

17

BACON HAD NO RESPITE when he resumed the Bruti deposition.

He was still mentally scarred from the previous mishap. Although he glared at Goon from time to time, he was methodical with Bruti, but not disrespectful. Gladys typed with one hand while taking out her false teeth with the other.

Larry called for a break and escorted Bruti out of the room.

Bacon took the opportunity for his own conference with Goon.

"You know what to do, Percy?"

"Prego, baby."

"Excuse me?"

Goon tapped his meathead. "It's in there. It's in there."

Larry re-entered with Bruti.

"Let's continue."

"Thanks for the honor, Herr Larry. Now, Bruti, let's go back to—"

Goon blitzed Bruti with a forearm to the temple. Fear froze Bacon and Larry. Bruti was, as the kids put it, knocked the fuck out.

*　　*　　*

WHILE THE PARAMEDICS revived Bruti, Larry scolded Bacon and Goon.

"If I didn't have respect for the Americans with Disabilities Act, I'd have my client sue your ass. But let me warn you. One more outburst and that's it."

Bruti flashed open palms. "Fine."

Larry winced, but nodded. "We reconvene tonight."

He left Bacon and Goon alone.

Bacon hobbled behind a seated Goon.

"I know you've gone through a lot in the past few days, Percy, but we can't afford these mental lapses."

"Right."

"Don't look so smug, Percy."

"I got it covered."

"Remember the process. I ask questions, he answers. The secretary takes a record and whatever he says can be used against him. If you beat him before he has a chance to answer, the secretary can't type anything we can use against him. Understand?"

"Completely."

18

PERCY TOOK A STUDY BREAK, roaming the streets of Geneva. All was well until he smelled a scent he couldn't place until an errant car alarm triggered a memory.

*   *   *

PERCY'S FIRST DAY at Canker had served as a harbinger of his future troubles. Canker's offices were located near the South Street Seaport in Manhattan. Although the fish market eventually had left the Seaport, decades of rotted seafood remained in the air. Right outside of the firm, Percy heard a car horn blaring. Ever nosy, he eventually found the source of the commotion—a fat fuck slumped over the wheel of a silver Bentley.

Most New Yorkers wouldn't care unless it was three in the morning or if they needed the parking space. Especially if street cleaning rules were in effect.

But it wasn't three in the morning and Percy didn't drive. He wanted to create some good karma on the first day of his Canker career.

Percy played Good Samaritan and ran inside the firm for help. It didn't take long for him to find a security guard. After all, every law firm perceived themselves as a terrorist target post 9-11 if they represented financial institutions, oil interests, or any of the bars George Bush's daughters frequented.

For a firm like Canker—which represented Japanese car manufacturers who had World War Two slave labor POW camps, Swiss Banks that defrauded Holocaust victim families, and Charlton Heston—it made no sense at all. Canker had hired a rent-a-cop anyway, to do what rent-a-cops do best: Not a goddamned thing.

It didn't stop Percy from expecting a miracle.

"Excuse me, sir. There's a dead man in a car outside."

"Really? What kind of car?"

"Excuse me?"

"What kind of car is this 'dead man' in?"

"I don't know."

"Why don't you check and let me know, okay?"

"But—"

The guard, who wore a nametag which read "JAKE", needed to muster every brain cell at his disposal. He only had two tiles left in Minesweeper. A false move would ruin five minutes of deep concentration. Percy understood the stakes just by looking at the guard's security screen, so he tiptoed back outside.

The horn still blared and no one cared but Percy. He performed a quick check on the Bentley. The fat man still slumped on the car horn, so Percy ran back inside and noticed the rent-a-cop glowing with pride. Before Percy could say a word, the security guard said, "Bentley, right?"

Percy nodded.

The rent-a-cop pulled up his pants, checked his zipper and went out to the Bentley. Percy asked, "Should we give him CPR?"

"Won't be necessary."

The rent-a-cop took a stun gun out of his pants and shocked the fat man, who shook, but still looked dead.

"What are you doing to him?"

He stunned him again, but to no avail. Percy went apeshit.

"Leave him alone! He's already dead!"

After one last tase, the fat fuck popped awake. The rent-a-cop sauntered back to 'work'.

Percy couldn't believe what he had witnessed. He'd watched Taser videos on-line, but a live tasing was quite another matter. It reeked of burnt barbeque, without the saucy goodness. Percy wanted to help the fat man, but was uncertain if the Taser electricity lingered. Percy didn't want to find out the hard way, so he looked around for something prod-worthy like a stick. As a germaphobe, he didn't want to catch a disease in the process. This was New York, after all.

Percy did the next best thing. He shouted at the top of his lungs. "Are you okay, sir?"

The fat man stirred and mumbled, "Jack…"

"You need Jack? A friend of yours?"

The fat man nodded and tried to utter some more.

"Dan…"

"Jack or Dan?"

The fat man shook his head and mustered the strength to beckon Percy closer. Percy sheepishly complied, still fearing a lethal cocktail of residual Taser electricity and germs.

"Who do you want?"

"Jack. Jack… Daniels."

The fat man gestured to the passenger side seat and an empty bottle of the famous Tennessee whiskey.

"I've… finished. Need… more. Please. I've… finished."

19

BRUTI WISHED HIS deposition was finished.

"How much longer is this gonna take?" Bruti groaned.

Tootie, a buxom babe who pecked the typewriter with her pinky, entranced a breast-comatose Larry.

Bacon snapped his fingers. "Larry, can I continue?"

Didn't work. Larry didn't know Bacon existed.

Tootie squeaked. "Wait a minute. I gotta finish typing."

They waited, but it was longer than a minute.

When Tootie finished typing, she clapped her hands. "Now I'm ready."

Bacon looked at her sideways. "Read me the last question asked."

"Let me see." She started reading, "'How much longer is this gonna take?'"

Bacon wiped his brow. "Not the questions I asked you. The questions I asked him."

She continued to read aloud. "'Can you speak more slowly since she can't type worth a shit?'"

Bruti pounded his lap. "What the fuck?"

Goon said, "Hey, it's gonna be fine. You want a brownie?"

"Actually, I do."

Goon nodded and whipped one out of his briefcase.

Spittle built up in the corners of Bacon's mouth.

"Percy, what the hell are you doing?"

Goon waved him away. "It's okay. Bruti, you feelin' better,

my friend? If not, just lemme know what you need."

Bacon barreled towards him.

"Larry, can I take a quick break?"

Larry was in another cleavage-filled world, so Bacon pulled Goon outside.

"What were you doing in there?"

"He looked hungry."

"We aren't supposed to be feeding him. We want him mad. Are you forgetting the plan?"

"I got a new plan."

"What?"

Larry scampered out the room with Bruti, leaving Bacon flustered.

"Larry, where are you going?"

"Sorry, Dick, but time is up."

"But we haven't—"

"We haven't thanked you enough." Goon glad-handed Bruti. "Sorry about the misunderstanding, man. It was these new supplements I'm taking."

"It's all good, son."

Bruti patted him on the back. "Take care of yourself, you hear?"

"Thanks a lot, man. You too."

He strolled away as Tootie emerged, chest puffed out, pleased with herself.

"That wasn't so bad."

"That wasn't so bad?" Bacon exploded. "You can barely type. You're virtually deaf and dumb."

"It's my first day."

"Well, get your pumps ready, hon. Once I'm done with you, you'll be back on the street turning tricks."

"What's your problem?"

"You are a slow, dim-witted, dumbass bitch. That's my problem, Tootie."

She bawled, but Larry came to her rescue.

"Back off, Dick. Can't you see she was trying?"

Goon continued to play peacemaker. "Larry, take this

cutie to dinner. On us." He handed the company credit card to Larry. "Here. It's the least we can do."

"Winkler, you're one class act. You could learn something from him, Dick." Larry escorted Tootie away and Bacon bristled with rage.

"Percy, I want you in my office tomorrow at the top of the morning. I need to go home, have a few drinks and try to calm myself down before we receive the transcripts tomorrow. I'll deal with you then. Calmly."

*　*　*

THE NEXT DAY, Bacon threw a fit, which didn't faze Goon.

"How can we possibly win, Percy? There's nothing in the transcript that will implicate him."

"Until we get the transcript and read it, how can we talk about it?"

"Are you retarded, Percy? Were you listening during that deposition?"

Someone knocked on the door. It was Tootie.

"And here she is. I hope the meal was good, Tootie. We paid for it after all."

She stuck her tongue out at Bacon and exchanged a book entitled 'BRUTI TRANSCRIPT' with Goon for a stack of Benjamins. Bacon seized the transcript from him and flipped through the pages.

"There must be a mistake. He admits to everything."

"I guess you kinda overreacted earlier and owe Tootie an apology."

Bacon was astonished by what amounted to a written confession.

"He admits to adultery? I never heard him say that."

"Baco-bits, you know that whatever you find in that transcript is admissible in court as prime face evidence."

"Prima facie."

"Exactly."

"Not if they object."

"Now, why would they do something like that?"

Bacon's phone rang.

It was Larry, who was sweating bullets while pouring over obscene photos featuring him as a gimp with midgets and Tootie.

"Dick, we got the transcript and don't have any objections." He forced himself to giggle. "No objections. So if you don't mind I have to go and handle other matters."

A large, black hand hung up Larry's phone.

A deep voice said, "Good job, my man. Now if you don't want these photos of your little escapade to find their way to the bar, your wife, or the *Times*…"

Larry said, "No, I don't want that."

The voice replied, "Don't want that, what?"

"Don't want that, sir."

"Me neither."

20

A SIGN FOR LAMB BURGERS at a Geneva gastropub inflamed Percy's sphincter. Not for a dislike of lamb or burgers. It reminded Percy of his second bar failure.

Canker had pulled Percy from the firm in an attempt to raise its public interest presence. Seemed perfect for Percy—he'd have time away from Bacon. Time to clear his mind. Refocus. And prep for the exam.

Canker removed him from the payroll and stripped him of his healthcare coverage. He didn't know where to go until Rufus hooked him up with Legal Advocates Making Bono—aka LAMB—a fifty-year-old nonprofit legal aid organization that provided programs and legal assistance for New York's indigent population. Harmony Lutz, LAMB executive director, understood his quandary and offered him a spot, glad to have a Columbia Law graduate under her wing.

As LAMB's Education Coordinator, Percy made presentations at pro bono 'beauty contests' held at law firms. They were called beauty contests since a number of pro bono organizations competed for the affection of corporate attorneys to volunteer whatever free time they had to help poor New Yorkers. It was an uphill task as most attorneys at law firms left work between eight and midnight. They left at eight if they didn't mind working on Saturday and Sunday. They left at midnight if they didn't want to work Sunday. With pressure like that, firm attorneys weren't receptive to working later. For free.

As a result, the pro bono organizations countered resistance to volunteer lawyering by touching whatever vestiges of humanity remained in the hearts of law-firm attorneys. Primarily through promotional videos filled with minority female victims—sometimes subtitled since the Ebonics and Nuyorican accents were so thick—and the SWM soul-wrenching attorney testimonials urging pro bono. Pro bono reps at the firm beauty contests also appeared in the videos, repeating the same points, observations, and jokes made in the flesh moments before playing their videos.

Percy watched the videos so many times he mouthed the words. It freaked him out—since he needed the memory space for bar study.

Firm attorneys left before Percy's presentation because the other presentations were so long. Some featured multiple staff members repeating the same points, examples, and figures as their co-worker presenters, with bitter consequences. Fights broke out amongst the presenters over ruined jokes and plagiarized war stories, making attendees feel like visitors at a divorcing couple's dinner table.

You know the feeling—wanting gravy to pour on your dry turkey, fearful to ask the husband to pass it, so you stare at your dinner roll. But it's dry, too. You just sit there, reminding yourself to get more info before accepting an invitation to a free meal that wasn't so free after all.

Some organizations served as havens for the hopelessly unemployable. When pro bono beauty contests took place during a firm-sponsored lunch, some cheap organizations sent entire staffs and their family members. For some it was the best meal they'd ever eaten. One family dressed in tiaras and tuxedo tails. The lunch was their night on the town.

The most popular pro bono organizations serviced wives abandoned or financially railroaded by their rich husbands. After winning massive financial settlements for these pro bono clients/victims, firms cultivated them as paying clients.

Every five seconds, 'interested' attorney attendees left, blaming their BlackBerrys after eating a free lunch. It amused

Percy, since firm attorneys earned enough to afford their own food.

Some firms had so many winding hallways with no seeming end Percy considered using breadcrumbs to mark the path. He knew that there were a few people still lost in the labyrinth of hallways and dead ends, like the guys in *Spinal Tap* or Jack Nicholson in *The Shining*.

Percy and his boss worked well together, until LAMB's Board of Directors canned Harmony for embezzlement.

Harmony's replacement was a real piece of work.

On his first day, he organized a staff meeting.

"My name is Mitch Jones. This place was a dump. I'm going to turn it around, so things are going to be different. This is not a forty-hour-a-week job. You will work nights and weekends if need be. There is to be no communication with the Board of Directors unless you first talk to me. When I give you a project, you are to give me daily progress reports for that project. Communication is key. If I don't see you, I don't know what you're doing."

As his new boss continued to lay down the law, Percy had Canker flashbacks.

"If you don't like it, there's always work at Starbucks. Any questions?"

*   *   *

WITHIN A MONTH, Percy was the only employee who wasn't fired and hadn't quit.

Mitch moved closer to LAMB and walked to work. He and Percy worked hard at getting things in order. So much so that after a point roombas could run the place. Mitch's job was such a sweet gig he feared the Board of Directors would find out and fire him. Just like Harmony. Mitch so feared attorneys overshadowing him, he replaced veteran attorneys with unqualified pre-law students.

Percy's burden was twofold. He did all the legal work in addition to putting out legal fires caused by inexperienced hires.

One would think that replacing attorneys who got paid

sixty-five thousand dollars with law students who received work-study would mean more dollars for existing staff. It did for Mitch, who raised his own salary to three hundred thousand dollars. Percy's thirty-thousand-dollar salary remained the same. He couldn't quit. Couldn't get a job until he passed the bar. So he worked his ass off to please Mitch. It made Percy a miracle worker.

Mitch had roaming anxiety with the predictability of a fiending crackhead. Calm at noon, anxious at one, ready to fire you at three, and best friends at four. He fancied himself many things. A gourmand...

"I don't eat much, so I make it count when I do."

A shaman with salves for headaches...

"Drink this. The horrid taste will pass. So will your pain. Namaste."

A graphic designer constantly dissatisfied with the graphical look of Percy's work product...

"Ever think of using a customized font?"

"For our tax forms?"

"I'm thinking if we used chartreuse, it might endear us to the IRS."

Another time, Mitch didn't care for the paper Percy used for a ghostwritten legal memo to the Bar Association.

"It's too, how do I say this, legal-looking."

Mitch whipped out a copy of *Wallpaper* magazine.

"I want all correspondence to have the feel of this magazine."

Percy thumbed through it. "This is an international design interiors magazine."

"It's sophistication. If we want people to respect the work we do, we need everything to look like this. Tell you what. Go to Takashimaya and buy some stuff that looks like this. Take it to Pierre, and have him make custom stationery for us. Here." He unsheathed his AmEx. "Use my card and keep the receipts. I need to be reimbursed."

Mitch had no life outside of work. He bragged about having had a girlfriend since third grade, even though Percy never saw one. Mitch had no friends, so he forced his employees to go shopping with him, watch movies with him, and purchase expensive front-row tickets to pro wrestling matches at MSG with him, even if they couldn't afford it.

How could you refuse? He was the boss.

The thing Percy hated most? Eating decadent delicacies. After eating a brownie, Mitch offered a cup of coffee. Percy wasn't a fan of the thick, syrupy concoction. If a friend or stranger gave it to him, he would've rejected it on the musty smell alone.

"Mitch, this is incredible."

"And one hundred and ten dollars a pound."

"You serious?"

"Only the best."

Percy tried different tactics to take it in without tasting. Too hot to gulp. Too pungent to tip and sip. He bit a hunk of brownie and chased it with as much coffee he could humanly muster, smiling with chipmunk cheeks. "What's the secret?"

"Civet shit. They eat the beans and shit them out."

Percy spat out his brownie coffee mush in his cup.

"Great idea, Percy." Mitch bit a hunk o' brownie, chased it with coffee, mushed it in his mouth, spat it in the cup and ate the regurgitated concoction with a tea spoon. "You are on to something, Percy."

Percy threw up a little in his mouth. Mitch pointed at his cup. "Eat up."

Percy rushed to the bathroom. Mitch rushed to eat Percy's coffee cud.

Even after he'd thrown up, the aftertaste lingered for hours. Two bottles of Listerine numbed Percy's tongue. He needed to numb his brain.

The next day, Mitch bragged of the other sick savories Percy had unknowingly digested working under him.

The tonic to cure his headaches? Baby mice wine.

That chewy stuff for stomach cramps? Kutti Pi? Goat fetus.

The Filipino street food appetizers served during Manny

Pacquiao fight that sounded like Baloo the bear? Duck fetus. Boiled alive. With no medicinal value whatsoever.

Of all the shit Mitch told Percy, Mitch failed to tell him the shit Percy needed to know.

Mitch's legal advice wasn't any different. He ranted about self-serving shit the clients didn't need to know. Ranted about Paris Hilton instead of giving advice on the lease the client had given him. He treated the client as a Paris Hilton surrogate. Percy covered for Mitch's narcissistic rants by giving practical advice.

Mitch realized that Percy was an asset: The ideal employee who made his boss look like gold. Mitch rewarded Percy by showing up to work late and leaving early each day.

About once a month, he'd surprise everyone by showing up to work early. God have mercy on you if you happened to be five minutes late on one of those days.

During a blizzard on a Friday, Mitch sent a BlackBerry message to staff that they could go home early. Since he'd sent the message from home, staff thought it was safe to leave. Percy had some work to finish up, so he stayed behind. At 5:30, Mitch came in to work.

"Percy, where is everyone?"

"They left, like you said."

"Call them back in."

"Call them back in?"

"If I'm here and I'm the boss, they should be here. It's only fair."

Mitch remained at work for another four hours.

One day, Columbia Law's Financial Aid Office called Percy, asking why he was in default of his loans.

"I am?"

"You sound surprised."

"It's the first I've heard of it."

"We've sent you a number of notices."

"I moved recently."

"No, to your work."

"I've changed jobs."

"You don't work for LAMB?"

"I do."

Turned out that Mitch was opening his mail. With no remorse.

Mitch said, "What are they going to do? You already spent the money on law school."

"Mitch, it's my personal—"

"At work, there is no expectation of privacy. Or didn't they teach you that at Columbia Law?"

"Yes, they did, but I thought—"

"Percy, I have to check your mail. I never know if the Board is trying to contact you, so I'm saving you the trouble of having to let me know if they do. It's not like I go through your bag, even though I have the right to if it's left open in your desk drawer."

Percy didn't know what to say.

"Percy, what time is it?"

"4:20."

"Shit, I'm late for spinning. Walk with me, will you?"

It was a ritual for Percy to walk Mitch to the gym, twenty-three blocks away from work, and in the opposite direction of where Percy needed to catch the train home.

Halfway to the gym, Mitch stopped walking.

"Damn it, Percy, I forgot to send an email to Tomkins. Could you go back to the office and do it for me?"

"Sure."

"Thanks. Plus, make reservations at the Ritz Carlton for the homeless talk at the end of the month. I don't wanna stay in a shithole when I travel to Outer Mongolia."

"We're talking about the non-profit coalition event in San Francisco?"

"So I'm supposed to slum it? It's not like I'm getting paid like these associates at law firms, you know."

"I do."

"They're paying one hundred and sixty thousand dollars a year for some asshole straight out of Columbia who isn't admitted to the bar."

"Yeah."

"You went to Columbia, so you know what I'm talking about."

"I do."

"Don't you hate how much they're getting paid? And for what? When I was at a firm, I was paid eighty-five thousand, and I didn't work any less than they are today. I'm sure when you were at a firm you were making one hundred and fifty thousand a year, right? And what do you have to show for what they put you through? Face it, bro. We're better off where we are anyway. I wouldn't want to have to sell my soul for that kind of money."

Mitch's BlackBerry buzzed.

"My painting is ready at Sotheby's. Could you do me a solid and pick it up before you go to work tomorrow?"

"Okay."

"Here are the keys. I'm having the place cleaned tomorrow, so make sure you keep an eye on that non-dusting bitch Slovak who busted up my armoire last week."

"Sure."

"And to think, I'm paying her even though I'm doing the dusting myself. Help these days. If we were making big money, we'd be able to afford good help, right?"

"I clean my own apartment."

"Oh no. I haven't made a bed. Ever. I'm not going to start today. I'll make sure I mention that to the Board while we're up for pay raises. I think I can get you up to thirty-two thousand this year from your thirty thousand."

"Thanks."

"But I'll have to justify it somehow. Maybe if you start working on Sundays."

"I have to study for the bar in a few weeks."

"I'm not paying you to study, Percy."

"I know that, but—"

"Look, you already failed once, and it was a mistake. It should be a cakewalk the second time around. You went to Columbia Law, after all."

"What about the month off?"

"I was going to talk to you about that anyway. You can't take a month off. It's too much time away from work."

"But it would be my unused vacation time."

"You only have one day of vacation."

"I have a month."

"You accrue vacation."

"That's not what Harmony told me when I accepted the job. In fact, it's the only reason why I accepted the job, because I could take time off to study."

"Look, if you're not at work, it puts a burden on everyone else."

"I have a plan for that. Shelby can—"

"Shelby can what? Do your job? If we can do your work, why does it even make sense to have you working in the first place? I mean, not to be a prick, but what do you do all day, anyway?"

Percy couldn't believe he was having this conversation with Mitch. After all the time Percy spent, he thought he deserved a little respect.

"I do a lot, Mitch."

"Apparently not, if Shelby can do your work."

"My work would be spread around."

"So I have to do your job in addition to my own? Will I be getting your salary, too? I won't. And for what? So you can just take off and study for the bar? I'm going to Spain during that time."

"I thought you just came back from hiking in the Amazon last week?"

"I'm the boss, Percy. What I do with my time isn't any of your business."

"Sorry."

"Look, I'll think about it, but I can't give you any more than a day."

"A day?"

"I think I could get a temporary attorney to come in during that time. Lord knows how busy I am."

That night, Mitch called Percy at home.

"Look, I can give you a day and a half, tops."

"A day and a half?"

"I think it's fair."

"Uh—"

"I'm not trying to be a prick, but you can't just not come to work when you want. It affects everybody. People want to take vacation."

"I talked to Shelby and Nick and they were cool with it."

"Shelby and Nick aren't your boss, I am. And I'm telling you, it's a day and a half. Sleep on it."

He hung up.

Seconds later, the phone rang. It was Mitch.

"Don't forget to pick up the painting tomorrow. Thanks."

Later in the week, Mitch dropped Percy's healthcare in exchange for a week off work to study for the bar. Percy failed and was fired within a week for budget concerns. LAMB couldn't afford his thirty-thousand-dollar salary.

Percy understood.

When he learned that Mitch gave himself a thirty-thousand-dollar pay raise, he had a deeper understanding.

He returned to Canker and his Bacon butt-kickings resumed.

This time would be different. So he entered the Geneva gastropub and ordered the lamb burger.

Tasted like a burned bike tire.

21

BACK IN BACON'S OFFICE, Lance tried again to convince Bacon that Percy was not whom he seemed.

"Et tu, Lance?" Bacon replied.

"Percy was never that large."

"We have been over this before, Lance. He is on medication."

"What about his attitude?"

"It is clear that you have Percy envy, Lance, but Percy has been good to me. Our clients cannot get enough Percy. In fact, you are the only one who does not like Percy."

"But, sir—"

"Percy is here to stay. Now, if you continue to pester me about Percy, Lance, you might have to find another place to practice law. Am I clear, Lance?"

"Yes, sir."

"Good."

22

PERCY DECIDED TO RETURN to Manhattan the night before the exam. His practice test scores were horrid. Especially the Criminal Law and Procedure sections. His goody-goody past had emerged as a liability. Percy wished he'd either been a juvenile delinquent or watched more cop shows. But that was the past and he was in the present. Failing miserably.

Geneva hadn't helped, either. Too clean. None of the action or danger of Manhattan.

Percy hoped that going back to his apartment would enable him to absorb crime like a sponge. Plus, the last thing he needed was another train derailment derailing his exam.

Around the corner from his apartment, he visited a greasy spoon and stared at his utensils.

A voice from behind him said, "You're looking well."

Percy could have used a nice pair of Depends.

"Lance?"

"May I join you?"

"I just finished." Percy got up to leave. "Stay away from the fish nuggets." He gripped his stomach. "They bite back."

A waiter arrived with a veritable feast, including pie a la mode.

"Sorry for the wait, sir." He placed numerous culinary delights in front of Percy's humbled palate. "Enjoy!"

"You catch Ebola, Percy?"

"Ebola?"

"You've shrunk in what, five hours since I've seen you? You're not wearing a mask. It's good to see that in such a short time, there's no indication you've been in an accident."

"Right. My accident. Yeah, I made great progress today. I caught a parasite, which caused me to drop the weight, that's why I'm eating so much."

"Percy, I'm not sure I can say this on an empty stomach."

"Mi casserole es su casserole."

"I don't know what you did. I don't know exactly what you're up to, but that's what criminal investigations are for, right?"

He tapped Percy's face before walking out… not noticing Goon, who was so pissed at what he'd heard that he crushed a Bavarian cream donut inches in front of his gritting teeth.

23

PERCY DIDN'T SLEEP A WINK.

He tried a last-minute cram session, which wasn't working. When it finally was time to leave for the exam, Percy had no confidence he'd pass.

While waiting to enter the test site, Percy saw a photo of Lance on the cover of the New York Post. He read it aloud. "Cantankerous underage sex orgy for Canker lawyer?"

"Can I help you?"

It was a bar attendant who wore a nametag which read "Becky."

Percy smiled.

Becky sneered, "Your ticket?"

"My ticket? It's at work. But I've registered."

Percy started in, but Becky stopped him.

"No ticket, no entry."

"I left it at home."

"Then go get it."

He grinned. "Look, just let me in. I'll take the bar, go home and return with the ticket."

"You have ten minutes to go home and get it now."

"It's twenty minutes away."

"Do you want me to call security?"

"I don't have time for this."

She put up her dukes. "Wanna dance, tough guy?"

He waved her away and started past her. She responded with a tackle. And what felt like a sleeper hold. Her ability to easily (wo)manhandle him amazed Percy. He tapped and she shoved him out the door.

He brushed himself off and bolted back in. Only to be tossed out again.

Realizing the futility, Percy hailed a cab.

"The law firm of Canker Shore, please."

*　　*　　*

WHEN PERCY REACHED Canker, he handed the cabbie some bills before dashing into the building.

Percy scrambled to the elevator before a security guard stopped him.

"Identification, sir?"

"Stop fucking around, Jake."

He tried to pass, but Jake wouldn't budge. "What's your name?"

"You know my name, motherfucker. Percy Winkler."

"Right."

A booming voice came from the elevator lobby. "I'll be back in a sec, Jake."

It was Goon.

"Okay, Percy."

"Percy?"

"Yeah, that's Percy Winkler. You? I don't know."

"Rufus."

Percy juked Jake and entered an elevator as the doors closed.

Once he got out, he dashed to his office and upended everything to find his bar exam admissions ticket. He was having trouble finding it, so he had a coked-out associate help him in his search. Between Percy's adrenaline and the associate's coke rush, they were unstoppable.

The cokehead found the ticket.

"Got it!"

"Thanks. You're a lifesaver."

"So, um, what do I bill this under?"

"Miscellaneous Carmen Sandiego slash Where's Waldo Research."

"Kewl!"

Percy dashed to the elevator and bumped into Goon. They exchanged awkward glances before parting ways.

*   *   *

PERCY MADE IT back to the bar exam.

Took it.

And felt pretty good about his performance.

24

PERCY HEADED TO Canker the next day.

His office was intact. And the same as he'd left it.

"I'm here for you, Mr. Winkler." A strange man rushed Percy and took measurements.

"Mr. Bacon said you'd be smaller, but I had no idea you'd be this small."

Percy flashed a shit-eating grin. "Right."

"He said something about you being off your meds. Like Bane without venom."

"Bane as in Batman?"

"Exactly."

A familiar voice said, "My lord, Percy. You are but a fraction of your former self. No matter. The suit will increase your bulk." Bacon emerged.

Pimped out.

Instead of wearing black, grey, and navy blue British suits with dual vents and peak lapels, Bacon rocked brown velvet, red pinstripes on lavender, and FrozFruit chunky mango Bishop Don 'Magic' Juan wear with a green tie and a gold pocket square.

"Percy, I followed your instructions. To the letter."

Percy didn't know that alphabet. He knew Rufus had said things were handled, and handled they were. "Right. My instructions."

"Green is for the money, gold is for the honeys."

Percy gnawed his lips shut. Fearful of losing his new

kinship with Bacon if he busted a laugh.

"Do you like it, Percy?"

Percy nodded and bit harder when Bacon worked it like a dime-store supermodel. "Percy, this plan? Genius. Absurd at first, it makes absolute sense."

"What plan?"

"You don't remember?" Bacon stared at Percy's face. "Memory loss. The meds. Must be a side effect."

Percy grimaced. "Yes. My meds. Memory loss. Sorry, sir. I can't remember a thing."

"Let me remind you of brilliance once held. Currently, we represent client who are has-beens. We should shift our focus to clients in their prime earning years by going all in. Cultivating a style that makes us stand out as attorneys, but modeled after our prospective clients' heroes."

"Pimps?"

"Pimps, Percy. And who lacks love for a pimp?"

"A prostitute withholding money, sir?"

"Exactly. Non-paying clients will be guilted to pay, lest they be considered hoes. We gain the psychological advantage before we begin billing."

"We do?"

"We do. And you will follow 'suit' by wearing custom-tailored apparel. Like the fine garments for which you are being fitted."

"I can't afford this, sir."

"I've set up an account for you."

Great that Percy didn't have to use his own dime. Horrid as it'd make Percy a pariah. No Canker attorney fathomed working with a guy who dressed like an extra from *Superfly*. Still, it was a job.

"And this is but the beginning, Percy. I planned it all out when you were taking the bar. You shall dine at hip Manhattan spots that rap stars and athletes frequent."

"You've set up accounts there, too?"

"Sandy will give you a corporate card. You shall increase your visibility at the same establishments frequented by the

Knicks, Nets, Jets, Giants, and Rangers, so you can drum up business. In fact, if you believe you are in the presence of a professional athlete, you pay the professional athlete's tab."

Seemed sweet. Dressing like an idiot and living large on someone else's dime? A piece of flourless cake.

In theory.

In reality, Percy couldn't get a reservation to save his life.

When he did, maître d's wouldn't let him in. Turned out nobody dressed like Percy in his Technicolor Pimp Suits. He tried toning it down, but he wasn't cool enough to get in. Only way he got in? Going with Rufus.

The two visited Jay-Z's 40/40 Club, named after the rare group of Major League Baseball players who had recorded forty home runs and forty steals in a single season. When Percy arrived at the club, he saw a not-so-rare gaggle of groupies who probably slept with forty rappers and forty athletes in a single NBA All-Star Weekend.

The bouncers assumed Rufus to be a baller, so they escorted him and Percy to the exclusive 'Jay's Room'. Framed sports jerseys and a professional wrestling championship belt adorned the walls. The two sat on a white Italian leather wraparound couch and prayed no one would take advantage of the oversized bed that ran along the room perimeter. Rufus spied something in the distance, stumbled off the wraparound couch, climbed over the bed and rushed through the backdoor.

Percy was concerned, but his hunger was greater. The Cows-in-a-Blanket appetizers and Pizzitas bewitched him. Rufus popped his head back in and mouthed "Let's get the fuck out of here."

Percy couldn't leave. Jay's Room had an admission fee aka bottle service requirement. Didn't matter if he sat down for a minute. His ass had to pay.

He dropped five Franklins, took the bottle of Krug Rose, and started to bounce. Security stopped him again. Apparently, he couldn't leave with the bottle. Percy didn't want to waste champagne, so he tried to make it rain by spraying the crowd with bubbly.

The cork ended up hitting one of the groupies in the throat. On a normal person, that signaled instant death. But the groupie's throat had suffered so much abuse over the years, it had the resiliency of a trampoline. The cork's trajectory resembled a game of pinball: It ricocheted off her throat, bounced on a pair of fake boobs, caromed from a Brazilian butt lift, and eventually shattered a plasma screen television.

Percy would have been caught but for the fact that the lifted butt jiggled for five minutes after it was struck by the cork. All the bouncers were mesmerized by each Jell-O-like ripple from booty so big it looked like Michael Vick staged Chihuahua fights under her skirt.

The 40/40 debacle rubbed him the wrong way. Percy Winkler liked burgers at diners. Dive bars. Ray's pizza. All this fancy-schmancy shit didn't appeal to him. If Percy never saw Kobe steak for the rest of his life, he'd die a happy man. He tried frequenting fast-food joints that athletes endorsed, but the only time Eli Manning ate at Burger King was on TV.

Percy staged a farewell tour of his favorite stores and restaurants, dreading the fashion and culinary nightmares that awaited him with Bacon. Percy considered returning his old clothes, but his sweat stains had soiled them something fierce—so bad even thrift stores wouldn't accept them. He couldn't bear to keep his beloved clothes in his closet. They would serve as too-painful reminders of choices forsaken. Therefore, he, along with Rufus, bid farewell to his beloved garments via Viking funeral. He placed the clothes under piles of stone and soil on a boat, which was set afire in the Hudson.

Much lamentation was felt by Percy. Even more so when the coastguard forced him to dispose of the tumulus in addition to levying a hefty fine. Rufus convinced them that Percy wasn't engaged in a terrorist act and avoided the seemingly inevitable Homeland Security intervention.

A few days later, Bacon suggested Percy move into an

apartment off Central Park West. He figured if Percy lived amongst Bacon's targeted client base, he'd be more likely to get their business. Bacon wasn't subsidizing the rent, so Percy picked the cheapest place he could find.

It set him back four thousand five hundred dollars a month.

Percy feared an IRS audit if he claimed the business development expenses on his taxes. The final straw came two weeks later.

"Cornrows, Percy. On you. By the end of the week."

The timing couldn't be better for Percy. He'd get the bar results by the middle of the week. If he passed, he'd quit and continue living a cornrow-free life. No more Bacon. No more ass-whippings. No more bullshit. Percy wished hard.

And it partly came true.

There would be no cornrows. No more Bacon. No more ass-whippings. No more bullshit. Not because Percy had passed the bar.

Because he'd failed the bar exam. And Canker fired him the next day.

25

"REMEMBER WHEN WE first came here, Rufus?"

"In law school or the first two times you failed the bar?"

"Perseus and Bellerophon."

"They graduate with us?"

Percy pointed at a stone statute of a man wrestling a horse. "The sculpture?"

Rufus nodded. "Right. The sculpture."

"Reason versus irrationality."

Rufus squinted at the sculpture and puckered. "The guy's headless. How rational is that?"

"The horse is his head."

Rufus stood, arms akimbo, head tilting from side to side. "The horse is his head?" More head tilting.

Percy didn't know if Rufus was inspecting the statue or just cracking his neck. "You see it, Rufus?"

"Why is he wrestling with his head?"

"Perseus is reason."

"Who's Perseus?"

"The guy wrestling with his head."

Now it was Rufus wrestling with his head. "I thought that was Bolero."

Percy wanted to bolero Rufus. "Bellerophon. His horse. His irrationality."

"I thought the horse was his head?"

"It is. He's wrestling with himself."

Rufus wrestled with his earlobe.

Percy said, "It's the perfect visual representation of my problem."

"Instead of studying assault, just beat someone upside the head."

"And study from prison?"

Rufus beamed, inspired. "You'll have all the time in the world to study. And work out. Turn that bird chest into buffness. Think about it."

Percy leered, disgusted. "Just did. And no."

"Then don't beat them. Just push them. Hard."

"You're tripping."

"You're the one talking all of this horse head shit. But I'm the one tripping. That's rich."

Percy, fed up with the jibber-jabber, reacted maturely. By stomping his foot and sucking his teeth. "You gonna help me or what?"

"Chill out, homey. You bring your latest?"

*   *   *

RUFUS THUMBED THROUGH Percy's error-riddled mock Bar exam, rubbing his neck more intensely as he reached the end.

"Percy, what if I could hook you up with a weekend cram session that, if you survived, guarantees passage?"

"If I survived?"

Rufus wiped his fingers with a napkin. "Look, just forget I said anything about it."

Percy leaned in closer. "Too late."

Rufus balled up the napkin. "No. I can't say anymore."

Percy nabbed Rufus's napkin. "Come on, Rufus. The bar's next week. And my scores aren't getting any better."

Rufus snatched it back. "Percy."

"I'm broke. Have no job. No hope."

"Percy—"

"Please?"

Rufus stared at the napkin, scrunching it tighter, exhaling. Taking shallow breaths. "Okay. But this is just between us."

Percy popped up in his seat. "Solid."

Rufus crouched towards him, balled himself forward like the napkin he'd crushed earlier and lowered his voice. "I've done a lot of crazy things in my life, but this? It works. It really works."

"How much does it cost?"

"Cost?"

"The price. What's the price?"

Rufus rubbed his arms while looking around. "These people aren't just interested in money."

"These people? Who are these people?"

Rufus tilted his head towards Percy, eyes darting. "Put it this way—if I knew their real names it would be worth more than my life to say them out loud."

"For a review course?"

Rufus seized utensils while shaking his head.

"It's too dangerous."

"Dangerous lawyers? This I've gotta see."

"Who said they were lawyers?"

Rufus spotted a figure spying through the window.

"I gotta go."

Rufus dumped his utensils, stumbled, and rushed through the backdoor.

Percy was concerned, but his hunger was greater.

26

OUTSIDE THE RESTAURANT, Rufus rubbed the sides of his cellphone. Should he pull the trigger? His stomach churned and he decided against it. Soon as he put the phone away, he felt it vibrate.

"What's the chance?"

Zero. No one had called.

Soon as he put it back, he felt it ring again.

Still no one had called. So he looked at his contact list, worried about exercising the nuclear option. Percy needed help. Help he wouldn't need if Rufus hadn't...

No time for that. Rufus didn't have a time machine.

He had a number. A way out. A chance that could be the greatest thing for Percy or his worst nightmare.

Could Percy handle it?

Rufus rubbed the sides of his cellphone. Should he pull the trigger? His stomach churned and he decided against it.

Soon as he put the phone away, he felt a tingle in his front pants pocket. Pulled out his phone. No one had called.

He knew what he had to do.

27

WHEN PERCY ARRIVED home, he saw a piece of paper stuck under his apartment door.

"The fuck?"

It had a phone number and the words "CALL ME" on it.

He called.

Within the half hour, he wished he hadn't.

28

PERCY WISHED HE'D NEVER called that number.

But how could he refuse?

It had been there. In his apartment. Practically begging to be called.

A phone number.

He didn't know who'd given it to him. Had no clue who he was calling. He'd just called.

And within the hour, they'd come.

Just like that.

29

"MAN, IT REEKS IN HERE."

"What's up with these clothes?"

"We'll find out soon enough, dumbass."

"Who you callin' dumbass, dumbass?"

"Yes! Yes! Yes!"

"No. No. No."

"Yes! Yes! Yes!"

The nattering woke Percy from his slumber. His head felt heavy.

Last thing he remembered? Answering the door and having a wet rag shoved up his nose.

His nostrils felt dry now. He grabbed his sides and gripped his arse and felt comfort that his kidney and virginity remained intact.

His comfort didn't last long. Something pinched the base of his neck. Something hard, weighing it down. He tugged at it.

A chain?

Not just any chain. A gold chain. Eighties, Run-DMC, rapper-style. Dangling from his chest atop a black robe like a judge's.

His head still felt heavy. And covered.

Soon as he scratched his itchy scalp, white powder flew everywhere like he was trapped in a snow globe. Filled with unknown chalkiness that threatened every orifice.

He froze and flashed back to that summer when envelopes

of white powder terrorized the city.

Percy held his breath, pinched his nose and hyperventilated.

Then he realized that if it was poison, he needed to expunge it from his system. So he hacked and snorted, blew and chortled. Until he realized his head felt heavy because *something was on it.*

Percy clucked like a chicken. It plopped off his head and landed in a cloudy mess on the ground. Once the powder cleared, he recognized the white, powdered, curly locks.

A judge's wig? I'm wearing a judge's wig. And a robe? What kind of moot court from hell is this?

Then it struck him.

Maybe it's some kind of judge cosplay? With hot young ladies dressed as bailiffs? Or court transcribers? This better not be one of Rufus's parties.

He wiped his eyes clear, blinked rapidly as he scanned the room, and spied six others dressed just like him—two irate Abercrombie-looking dudes comparing their robes; a sour-faced ethnically-ambiguous gal dry-washing her hands while sizing the Abercrombie Bros up; an intense guy sizing up the floor while chanting "Yes"; a hygienically-challenged woman with white-girl "dreads" hanging underneath her powdered judge's wig mouthing "No"; and a nerd with baby teeth gnawing his fingernails.

Percy sneezed at the mustiness, his skin all itchy from powder.

A door opened and roughnecks dressed like *Grease* rejects wearing Robin masks pranced in snapping. Percy didn't know if they were members of a Sha Na Na revival or a local *West Side Story* production.

Behind them waddled a large black man wearing a pirate eyepatch and a varsity jacket with the name "Pledgistopheles." Looked like the bastard child of Bigfoot and Precious. Hair all conked with remote control in hand.

"All of you retards are here for one reason: You can't pass the bar. We got a one hundred percent guarantee that you pass. And if you don't pass, I lose my one hundred percent guarantee, and you lose one hundred percent of your ass. You did it your way and failed. Miserably. So now?" He started singing Frank Sinatra's *My Way*.

His goons clapped and hooted.

The "Yes"-chanting psycho clapped and whistled with them. The dreaded girl whimpered. Percy scratched the back of his neck.

The nail-munching nerd made a mad dash for the door. Pledgistopheles raised the remote control at him, aimed and pressed a button with a fat finger.

"Bang."

The gold chain around the nerd's neck hummed and shook. The nerd panicked and the chain smoked. He convulsed. Sparks popped from his robe. The white wig on his head turned flush with crimson. Piss streamed from the robe and he flopped on the ground.

Dead.

"Anybody else got someplace better to go?"

Nope.

"Good. This is the last weekend before the bar, so we're gonna do a little cram session."

Percy couldn't keep his eyes off his gold chain. It felt a little warmer than before. He scrambled to put his wig back on as Pledgistopheles lectured.

"Every hour, you get a bag. In the bag, you find a job you gotta do and the tools you need to do it. You don't do the jobs? You die. You snitch? You die. You get locked up? You die. Capisce?"

The dready girl blubbered. Pledgistopheles put an unwelcomed arm around her.

"You must be Bridget. It's okay, hon. I'm just helping you study."

One of the Abercrombies tittered. "Helping us study? By scaring us half to death?"

Pledgistopheles pinched at his nose. "I'm sorry. Let me be specific. Kent, right?"

He nodded. Pledgistopheles flashed a shitty grin. "Instead of studying assault, you're gonna bust some motherfucker upside the head."

Kent's face tightened.

Pledgistopheles steepled his fingers beneath his chin. "Too extreme? Then give a little love tap. Or a hard shove."

Percy recognized the words, but couldn't place them.

The "Yes" weirdo cackled and caressed his gold necklace. Pledgistopheles pointed at Percy.

"You know how the bar works, right?"

Percy, lost in the moment, didn't see Pledgistopheles pointing at him.

Pledgistopheles flapped his hands at Percy.

"Hey, you. Tell us how the bar exam works."

Percy cleared his throat. "Excuse me?"

"You heard me. What the fuck is on the bar exam?"

Percy closed his eyes. Took a calming breath. "Random scenarios with legal issues."

Pledgistopheles raised the remote from hell at Percy. "Like what?"

Percy loved life too much to go out like the electrified nerd. Something in his brain clicked.

He became Robo Nerd.

"Johnny, an adult, has intercourse with Susie and doesn't know she's sixteen. During rough sex, she dies. Is Johnny guilty of A, statutory rape, B, murder, C, felony murder, D, A and B, or E, none of the above?"

Pledgistopheles nodded. "Easy one to visualize, Kent? Since you're into young girls and rough sex."

The weirdo guffawed. "More like gerbils up his ass."

Pledgistopheles continued. "Point is, finer distinctions of the law are harder to visualize, so you'll act them out."

"That's it?" Kent sneered.

Pledgistopheles smirked. "That's it."

Kent's face scrunched, dried lips cracked and puckered. "Trent, what the fucks are we doing here?"

Trent mimicked Kent's lemon face.

Pledgistopheles said, "Lemme give you an example. Dr. Cuddles, show us stop, drop, and roll."

A toothpick-chewing meathead with the name "Dr. Cuddles" embroidered on his jacket daintily extended his pinkies and twerked his booty. Stopped, dropped, and rolled. He sprang up, arms raised, pinkies still pointed skyward. Duck-lipped like a hoochie's cellphone self-portrait.

Pledgistopheles turned to Kent. "Your turn." He leered at Dr. Cuddles. "Without all that extra stuff."

Kent leered back. "As if."

"I get it. You wanna do the duck lips."

"I don't wanna do any of it."

Dr. Cuddles pulled a gun on Kent, who froze with fear.

"See, class? He knows what to do, but has performance anxiety. Some of you suffered the same calamity when you took the bar. Dr. Cuddles, you may proceed."

Dr. Cuddles lit a match and set fire to Kent's robe. It burned like paper.

"You shoulda bought the flame-resistant one, boss."

A flaming Kent scurried in circles.

"Stop, drop, and roll, motherfucker!"

Kent scampered while his robe smoked.

"Dr. Cuddles, proceed to the next step."

Dr. Cuddles shot Kent. Kent recoiled from the impact, stopped, dropped, and rolled.

Dead.

The room went silent. Eyes bulged, unable to blink. Chins and lips trembled. Heads shook in denial. Pledgistopheles fed off their fear.

"Now, ladies and gentlemens, please show me how to stop, drop, and roll. With duck lips and pretty tea-sipping pinkies."

They did.

"See? It works. Any more questions?"

Smoke billowed from Kent's lifeless body.

The weirdo chortled. "Any marshmallows?" He was the only captive who didn't look petrified. Percy didn't know what to make of it.

Pledgistopheles snapped his fingers.

"You study, sleep, and shit here. You only leave to do the jobs we give you. Anyone that ain't in this room tries talking to you? Ignore 'em. I'm your fucking world now. I know where you live, where your folks live, even the last website you jerked off to. I hear one peep that you rat me out and I pull an Abdul Gayribs on you."

Dr. Cuddles scratched his chin. "Abdul Gayribs?"

"You know. That towel-head torture joint? Black hoods, electrified nuts, and all that good shit."

Dr. Cuddles stroked his chin while nodding.

Pledgistopheles resumed his lecture. "Long as you do what I tells you, passing the bar will be as natural as morning wood. Trust me on this. You will be amazed by the beauty of our brutality."

Percy couldn't take his eyes off Kent's dead body. Rigor mortis set in. Pouty duck lips. Frozen forever as Kent's pinkies curled into bent meat hooks.

Dr. Cuddles whipped out a pair of x-ray specs before reading names off a notepad.

"Trent Vanderpoole."

Trent leered at Kent's corpse.

Dr. Cuddles threw a pencil at him. "Get over here and grab a bag."

Trent balled his fists.

Dr. Cuddles flashed a fiendish smile and met him nose to nose. His tongue scraped the back of his teeth. Back and forth. Like a metronome on speed. "Bring it, tough guy. I'm begging you. Avenge your friend. Be a hero and defeat Pledgistopheles and his fiendish minions."

Soul-sucking minions would've been more appropriate, since Dr. Cuddles sapped every drop of machismo from Trent. He responded with his hands raised, palms out. "I yield."

"You better yield your shit before I slurp the stuffing out yer wontons."

Trent left so quickly, his wig damn near fell off. He escaped with his bag—and more importantly, his wontons—intact.

Dr. Cuddles titled his head to the side. Cracked his neck. "Bridget Stanislaw."

Bridget twisted her dreads, staring at the body.

Dr. Cuddles repeated, "Bridget Stanislaw."

More staring. More dread-twisting. The crusty captive shoved her forward. Bridget awoke from fear-induced catatonia.

Bridget said, "Yes?"

"Now she talks. Get your fucking bag."

She did.

Dr. Cuddles read. "Stranger Lewis."

It was the "Yes"-cackling weirdo. Standing 'at attention' before marching to Dr. Cuddles and saluting him.

Pledgistopheles turned away from Stranger. "Not this motherfucker." He nabbed Dr. Cuddles's list. "Terminator Rex?"

Terminator Rex looked like the runt of the litter. Same height and slight build as Percy. Like his twin brother from a different mother.

Terminator Rex shot up. "Yeah, boss?"

"A word, please."

The two of them held a little conference as the weirdo remained at attention.

Pledgistopheles scratched his chin. "That isn't who I think it is, is it?"

Terminator Rex said, "I don't know. Who do you think it is?"

"Ask him, Rex."

Rex turned to the weirdo. "Asshole, who the fuck are you?"

The weirdo clicked his heels together. "Stranger Lewis, sir."

Pledgistopheles stomped towards Terminator Rex. "Of all the people, the fuck you let him in?"

"The fuck I let him in? To ask him one question." He turned to Stranger. "Asshole, I got a question to ask you."

"Sir, yes, sir!"

"How the fuck you get a name like Stranger?"

"My father, sir. That's how I got a name like Stranger, sir."

"Bullshit."

"No bullshit, sir. I didn't look like my father, so he named me Stranger, sir."

"Why not name you Mailman?"

"I didn't look like him either, sir. That's why I was named Stranger, sir."

"A comedian. At ease."

Terminator Rex whispered to Pledgistopheles.

"What do you think now?"

"He'll either be great or a hot stinking pile of donkey shit."

"We keep him?"

"He paid his money?"

Terminator Rex nodded. Pledgistopheles grimaced. "He paid his money." He wiped his eyebrows in place. "Okay." He poked the back of his bottom gums with his tongue. "Stranger?"

"Sir, yes, sir."

"Pick up your bag and skedaddle."

"Sir, yes, sir."

Stranger strutted to Dr. Cuddles, took the bag, and did a familiar dance.

Pledgistopheles said, "The Truffle Shuffle. God damn it, Rex, you're responsible for that crazy fuck. You got me?"

"Sir, yes... I mean, yeah, boss."

"Keep reading, Dr. Cuddles."

"This can't be right."

"What?"

Dr. Cuddles handed the list to Pledgistopheles.

"This a typo?"

The crusty lass marched forward with a pinched mouth.

Pledgistopheles read, "Sif? Like Thor's girlfriend?"

Dr. Cuddles pursed his lips. "Thor?"

Pledgistopheles said, "You know. God of Thunder. Fucks people up with a hammer."

"Oh, that Thor. With the hammer."

She bit her inner cheek meat. "No, Syph. Like Syphilis."

Pledgistopheles stomped and hissed.

Dr. Cuddles giggled like a schoolgirl. "What the fuck were your parents thinking?"

She said, "It's a long story."

Dr. Cuddles couldn't help himself. "I guess it could've been worse. Then again, no. It couldn't be any worse than that. Syphilis. That's a good one."

She took her bag and stomped out. Dr. Cuddles still snickered.

Pledgistopheles hated Snickers. He was a Tootsie Roll man. "Dr. Cuddles, the fuck's the problem?"

"Sorry, boss, but that chick's name is Syphilis."

"I heard."

"Like the disease."

"I'll make you wish you had a disease if you don't do your goddamn job, asshole."

"My bad, boss." He resumed reading. "Let's see. Kent Fullsworth."

Nobody answered.

"Fullsworth?"

More silence.

"Oh yeah. I forgot."

He tossed the bag on Kent's corpse and read the next name.

"Percy Sphincter."

Percy cowered forward. "It's Winkler. Percy Winkler."

Pledgistopheles's eyes lit up. "No kidding? Like Da Fonz?"

For the uninitiated, Da Fonz, AKA Arthur Herbert Fonzarelli BKA Fonzie, was a character in the popular seventies sitcom *Happy Days* played by Henry Winkler, in front of a live studio audience. *Happy Days* romanticized America in the fifties.

Fonzie epitomized cool. He wore a leather jacket, rode a motorcycle, illuminated lights in a room by snapping his fingers. No clap-on, clap-off clapper, either. This was pre-clapper.

Fonzie started car engines by banging the hood with his fist. Viewers worshipped Fonzie and aped saying "Aaay!" like Da Fonz, clicking their fingers and forming thrust-forward double thumbs up.

Percy half-assedly stuck one thumb up at Pledgistopheles. "Yeah. Like the Fonz."

"Then you don't mind if we call you Fonzie."

Dr. Cuddles picked up the joke and imitated the Fonz. "Aaay!"

Percy widened his eyes. "No. I don't mind." A part of Percy died inside.

Pledgistopheles slapped Percy's back. "Good. Coz Percy's a faggot name. We gonna get along just fine."

Dr. Cuddles couldn't get enough of the Fonz. "Aaay!"

Percy flashed a nervous tic while picking up his bag. Then he thought about it.

What am I doing here? This is craziness. The Sopranos *meets* Happy Days? *As a bar prep? Who could have set me up with this? Does it matter? I'm here now. And I have to say something.*

He turned to Pledgistopheles.

"Excuse me, sir. There must be a mistake." Percy put on his puppy-dog face.

Pledgistopheles put on his pit-bull face, which didn't differ much from his normal look. "A mistake?"

"Yes, sir. I shouldn't be here."

"You ain't Percy?"

"Yes, sir, I am."

"Good, now get the fuck to work."

Pledgistopheles walked away.

Percy's heartbeat raced. He bit down on his bottom lip. *Focus. Come up with an excuse.* It came to him. "I don't think I'm going to take the bar anyway, so I really don't need this class. But thanks for the opportunity. You really seem to care.

And that makes me care."

Pledgistopheles kept walking.

Percy's chest tightened. *Balls-to-the-wall time.*

Percy exhaled. "I didn't pay."

Pledgistopheles stopped in his tracks.

"You didn't pay?"

"Nope."

Pledgistopheles tilted his head. Gave Percy a once-over. Beads of sweat formed on Percy's head. Pledgistopheles smiled politely, not genuinely. "Terminator Rex, sign Fonzie up for one of our payment plans."

Terminator Rex ran the numbers in his head. It seemed epic, like he wrote each number in the sky with his eyes. Would've set the roof afire if he had heat vision like Superman. "Twenty grand?"

Pledgistopheles looped his fat thumbs into loaded front pockets. "Sounds fair."

Dr. Cuddles pitched a bag into Percy's chest. "Go time, Fonzie."

How about 'go home' time? Look at this crap. These clothes. These bags. These nutjobs.

That number.

Who the fuck gave me that number? I shouldn't have called. Man, I shouldn't have called. But I had no choice. It was there. And I'm here. And they know about the bar. That means these psychos know somebody I know. But who?

Percy cycled through his mental rolodex. It wasn't extensive.

It didn't matter.

All it took was one person. One major asshole to do this to him.

30

PERCY STUMBLED OUTSIDE of Pledgistopheles's without looking back. Physically, that was. Mentally, he still stewed, still not knowing who'd given him that number. That horrid number.

Mother wouldn't set me up with this. She's too cheap. Couldn't be Columbia. I still owe them money. Unless they added it to my bill? How else are they gonna get a return on their investment unless I pass the Bar?

He stared at his robe.

Nah. I'm in the one percentile of graduates who haven't passed. No way they'd shell out this kind of coin for perfection. Still...

He looked around for inspiration. Some insight.

Then he set his eyes upon the place he just exited.

A frat house?

Not just a frat house. The only house on the block.

Why is it a frat house?

Percy had never pledged. He didn't like people telling him what to do and the thought of hazing didn't appeal to him. He'd end up getting hazed at Canker, but that story will have to wait.

Percy fixated on the frat house o' horror as he backed up with uncertain, drunken steps.

Right into Syph.

In mid-sentence.

She shoved him away and crafted a new one. Just for him. "Back the fuck up, sack-muncher."

Trent's lips flattened. "Why couldn't it have been him instead of Kent?"

Percy rubbed his forehead. "Who's Kent?"

"His extra-crispy homeboy." Stranger chuckled. "Come to think of it, I've never seen white bread that toasty."

Trent got in Stranger's face, fists balled, nostrils flared.

Stranger smacked himself in the head while making monkey noises.

Syph separated them. "Calm the fuck down, assholes."

Trent spat on the ground before backing off. Stranger peeled an imaginary banana, wiped it in Trent's grounded spit, and ate said imaginary spit-dipped banana. He enjoyed every bite with exaggerated chewing, finger-licking, and lip-smacking.

Syph violently rolled her shoulders forward. "Like I was saying, if we don't commit all of the elements of a crime, we're fine."

Percy's head flinched back slightly. "Like what?"

"Like this." Stranger snatched Bridget's purse. She was too dazed to care. "Am I guilty of robbery or larceny?"

Percy tugged on his bottom lip. "Larceny."

Trent folded arms across his chest. "He used force, so it has to be robbery."

Syph gritted at him. "It's neither."

Stranger tossed the purse back at Bridget. It smacked her in the face. Stranger smirked. "I lacked the mental intent to permanently deprive her of her property."

Syph's eyes darted about. "We keep on our toes and avoid arrest? We'll be good to go."

Percy leaned in. "We can slip out of town while they're not looking."

Syph leaned in closer. "You feel that knob on the necklace?"

He did.

Syph cupped her mouth with her hands while whispering, "It's probably a little camera."

Percy shuffled back a step. "Spyware? They can see and

hear everything?" He freaked. "Like I said, Pledgistopheles is dressed so well and classy, let's do whatever he says."

Syph roared. "Just fucking with you. It's a glorified GPS with remote death shock."

Percy said, "How'd you know that?"

"I saw a movie about this kinda stuff."

Trent winced.

Stranger pulled out a tire iron and a pair of pantyhose from the bag. "If you'll excuse me." He pulled the pantyhose over his head like a mask, the panty crotch over his face, thrust his chest out and strutted away. "Aggravated assault, here I come."

Before Percy caught his breath, Syph grabbed him.

"We got a conspiracy to commit." She pulled out a map from her bag. "You recognize this area?"

"Nope."

She scanned the map. He tugged his wig. "Where are we?"

"According to this, near some bullshit, nothing-happening college I never heard of in boonies."

"We still in New York?"

"Does it matter? We're here." She pointed ahead. "Campus is a few blocks away. Some housing project is to our left. Commercial strip is in the other direction."

"So which way are we going?"

"You stay here while I handle things."

"What about her?" Percy pointed at Bridget.

Syph buzzed her lips. "What about her?" She stared at the map. Walked quickly. With purpose.

Percy caught a glimpse of Bridget, staring into oblivion, crushed like a nut sack in a West Village S&M parlor.

An appropriate analogy given the frat house. And the swift kick in the nuts he'd felt upon arriving.

Hazing.

A chill shot down his spine so hard, his toenails almost clawed through his shoes.

How the fuck did I end up in here?

Percy's heart raced. His mind flooded with memories.

It hit him.
Doesn't matter. I'm here. Regardless of why. Or whom.
Be the beaver, Percy. Mentally dam that shit. Stick by stick.
More calming breaths.
Stick by stick, Percy. One at a time, Percy. One at a time.

31

"I'VE FINISHED, PERCY."

Syph stared at Percy's dazed ass. She snapped, "Yo, Percy."

Percy stirred himself awake. He needed to focus on Syph. With a new gym bag still with sales tag attached.

"Where'd you get that, Syph?"

"Don't worry about it. Just follow me so we can do this conspiracy job." She jogged away. A clueless Percy, fumbling with his robe, barely kept up.

"What are we conspiring to do?"

"Larceny."

"I don't know if I can do this."

"All we need for a conspiracy is an agreement to violate the law."

"Great."

"So do you agree?"

"Agree to do what?"

"To violate the law."

"What if we get caught?"

"Just say I put a gun to your head."

"But you didn't."

Syph whipped out a pistol and held it to Percy's temple. Water dripped from the spot where gun met wig. Not water from sweat. Water from the 'gun.'

"Pledgistopheles wouldn't give us real guns. But you get the point, right?"

He didn't. "Sure. Now what are we supposed to do?"

"'We' aren't doing shit. You're staying here since you'll probably fuck it up. Just watch my bag."

"No problemo, Kemosabe."

She rolled out.

Percy put the bag between his legs under his robe. He looked like he had a giant hard-on poking out.

Percy couldn't keep his eyes off the bulge, I mean bag.

What's inside? I gotta know, but can I look?

Percy damn near broke his neck looking around for witnesses.

Someone might be around. Peeking. All nosy and shit.

He didn't see anyone.

What if Syph catches me looking? She did tell me to keep an eye on her bag. Does that include the insides?

Percy shook the bag. Sounded like something was loose inside. *Hopefully nothing explosive. Otherwise—*

He stopped shaking it. And started squeezing it.

That might cause an explosion, too.

He stopped. Checked around for Syph.

Maybe if I count to one hundred, I can look.

Sure enough, he started counting.

After reaching thirty-four, Percy checked if the coast was clear. He removed the bag from between his legs. Unzipped it.

"Jesus Christ!"

Baggies with white powder. Hastily wrapped foil nuggets, dripping with white powder.

Drugs?

Lots of them. In baggies and foil. Percy had never smuggled drugs, but he'd seen enough television to know what drug smuggling looked like.

But this wasn't television. Shit was for real. Percy saw *Oz* flash before him.

I can't just stand here. I gotta move. Myself or the bag. Maybe hide it behind a tree? Under a bench? Under my robe again?

Before Percy could act on his neurotic impulses, police

lights flashed from the street.

A voice over a loudspeaker shouted. "Put the bag down, frat boy."

It was the cops.

32

PERCY'S BACON WAS COOKED when the cops ordered him to freeze. Busted? So soon? If Pledgistopheles found out, Percy would be toast. Fear took his breath and legs, so running wasn't an option.

After inhaling deeply, he said, "Officer, I don't understand why this is—"

The cop clutched Percy by the collar of his robe. Another cop entered the fray.

"This the mule we've been looking for all night?"

Percy did a double-take. "Mule?"

One cop inspected the bag. "What do we have here? Monty, you got that thing?"

"What thing?"

"That coke-testing thingamajig."

"Didn't you bring it?"

"Fuck."

"Don't get mad at me, rook."

"Rook? You've been on the job two months longer than me."

"That's two months longer than me, *sir*."

Percy spazzed out. "You've got it all wrong."

"We do?"

Percy said, "It's not my bag."

The senior cop said, "Whose is it?"

Percy said, "Syphilis."

The rook said, "You have Syphilis?"

Percy said, "Syphilis left."

The senior cop said, "You had Syphilis, but you're cured?"

Percy said, "Syphilis is the woman responsible for this. It's hers."

The rook said, "A woman. Named Syphilis?"

Percy said, "Yes."

The senior cop said, "What's her mother named? Ghana Rhea?"

The rook said, "Where is she right now?"

Percy said, "Committing a larceny."

The senior cop said, "Excuse me?"

Percy was lost for words. "A larceny of the heart." It was the best he could think of, until he added mustard.

"I'm in love."

The senior cop grabbed the back of Percy's neck. "Let's book him."

Percy tensed up. "You can't take me in. Look, I can make this worth your while."

The senior cop said, "You bribing us?"

Percy said, "I wouldn't dare think of it. Unless—"

The cops dragged him away.

"No, you can't." Percy remembered his necklace. GPS, maybe? Probably would show him going to the police station. Pledgistopheles would fry him remotely. That was if he was still in range. Maybe he'd blow up automatically as soon as he left a certain radius? It wasn't a risk Percy was willing to take. He needed to stay put. Needed to say something. "Why arrest me now when I can get you the big boys?"

The senior cop said, "You're gonna rat on your boys?"

Percy said, "Yes, but I need your help with some shit. And man, is it big."

The senior cop said, "How big you talking about?"

Percy said, "Just let me go and—"

The rook said, "And what?"

"If you arrest me, what'll it do for your careers? Wait until Monday. After that, you'll be heroes."

The senior cop shoved Percy forward. "Move it, buddy."

The rook raised an open palm. "Wait a second, Monty."

Monty said, "Butch."

Butch pointed at the bag. "All the drugs? They had to come from somewhere."

Monty shrugged. "We didn't even test them."

Butch said, "Fuck the test." He nabbed a baggie, opened it and shoved it in Percy's face. "Snort it."

Percy scratched his wig. "Exsqueeze me?"

Butch smacked the back of Percy's wig. "You heard me. Like an anteater. Only with coke instead of bugs."

Monty grabbed Butch's shoulder. "Butch, this is wrong."

Percy nodded at Butch. "He's right, Officer Butch."

Monty aped Percy's nodding. "That's right, Butch. You're wrong. Anteaters eat with their tongues. Like this." He poked out his tongue, then retracted it. In and out. Slurping.

Butch smacked his hip. "Right." He copied Monty's anteater impression with his tongue curled. "See? Like this, I can catch more ants."

They engaged in a mock ant-eating competition. Dueling tongues poked, wagged, and slurped imaginary ants.

Butch said, "You're eating little ants. I'm eating the big ones."

Monty said, "Fuck your ants. Mine are chocolate-covered."

It sent Butch into a tizzy. "My ants have chocolate sundaes with sprinkles on their backs, tough guy."

Monty replied, "My ants are hot female Amazon ants. With tits. And I'm doing the doo with them."

"Not anymore." Butch jumped in front of Monty and copulated with his ants. "How you like them apples? I mean, ant-ples?"

They engaged in a virtual Kama Sutra competition with their imaginary ants.

"Wow. That's pretty kewl. You're anteaters. Eating ants." Percy wanted to disengage these clowns.

Monty flashed his piece at Percy. "Your turn."

Percy, cottonmouth dry from fear, could barely open his

mouth much less stick his tongue out. "It's stuck."

Monty pouted and stomped. "I hate when this happens."

The cops each stuck out a fist. Percy flinched with fear.

The cops shook said fists. "One, two, three, shoot."

Monty had rock. Butch had paper.

Monty stomped towards Percy. "Goddamn it. This is your fault. Remember that."

Percy didn't know what Monty planned to do, but begged anyway. "You don't have to do this."

Monty shrugged his shoulders and took a plastic baggie of coke.

Butch leered at Percy, daintily extended a pinky and scooped.

The radio went off in the police car, jolting Butch.

"Calling all available units. We have a situation on Lorraine near the lot. Backup requested like pronto. I repeat, backup requested immediately and shit."

Butch wiped off the coke on Percy's robe. Monty backed up towards the car. "The fuck is going on in this neighborhood tonight?" He put on gloves, whipped out a sheet of paper, wrote something on it, and handed it to Percy. "Read it."

Percy took it and read. "'I did it?'"

Monty pointed at Butch. "You hear that?"

Butch winked. "Copy that."

Percy scratched his head. "Copy what?"

Butch snatched the paper away. "Your confession." He shook the paper. "Along with prints."

Monty snapped a cellphone picture of Percy. "And photo. Nice doing business with you." He took the bag o' drugs and strutted to the car.

Butch still advanced towards Percy with bad intentions. Or constipation. Whatever the inspiration, it didn't look good to Percy.

Monty pounded the car roof. "Butch, vamoose."

Butch stopped, stared at Percy and walked to the car. Backwards. "Got my eyes on you, fucker. Oh yeah. Right on you." He stuck out his tongue anteater-style, wagged it left to right and slurped the last imaginary ant.

Once in the car, they peeled out. Percy needed to pee out. And kinda already had.

Percy fingered Pledgistopheles's chain. Percy's umbilical cord. Feeding Percy's fear, Percy's hopelessness. Visions of a showdown between the cops and the goons flashed before him. Percy caught in the crossfire. What could he do? Wait for Syph? Tell Pledgistopheles?

Don't just stand there, Percy.

"Who's there?"

We have to go.

"Go where?"

Chop, chop, Percy.

"The fuck's wrong with you, Percy?" Syph shoved him, clearing his cobwebs.

"I confessed."

"Confessed what?"

"Crimes. Confessed crimes."

"They read your rights?"

"Doesn't matter."

"The fuck it doesn't."

"They threatened me. Said they'd... they'd..." Percy blubbered.

Syph had no pity for the fool.

"You can't waive your Miranda rights under the threat of force, Percy. So get over it."

"They found drugs."

She laughed.

"What's so funny?"

"The drugs. They test 'em?"

"They scooped it out and almost—"

Syph wiped the white residue from Percy's robe and shoved it in his mouth.

He tried spitting it out, but it was too late. Blood flowed rapidly throughout his body.

Syph smirked. "You feel that rush, Percy?"

Percy tottered like a bobblehead, eyes fluttering like a moth on meth.

"Syph, I've never—"

She placed a finger over his lips. His heart raced.

"Syph, my heart is palpitating." He convulsed. "I think I'm overdosing." He gripped his chest, clutched his robe, tongue wagging. "Help. Please."

She slapped the taste out of his mouth.

"It's sugar, you nitwit."

"But I thought—"

"Thought what? A panic attack was an overdose?"

"But the cops—"

"Won't do shit. I went to a grocery store when I first left you. Bought some aluminum foil, baggies, sugar and chocolate."

"You mixed chocolate with the drugs?"

"The foil had chocolate in it, not heroin."

"And the coke?"

"Sugar, motherfucker."

"Oh. But still—"

"Unless there's an A.P.B. for making the world taste good, you'll be fine, Candyman."

33

INSIDE THE FRAT HOUSE, Dr. Cuddles passed out test booklets.

"Practice test time."

Percy fixated on his encounter with the cops and Syph. His scalp itched, probably bumping up like his arms, red from rubbing the robe. Contact dermatitis, maybe?

How could he take a test under these circumstances? Didn't seem to affect anyone else but him and Bridget, who stared at the frat house entrance.

A woman dressed like Percy and his fellow 'pledges' rushed into the room. "Sorry I'm—"

The gold chain around her neck hummed, shook, and smoked. She convulsed. Sparks popped from her robe. She flopped on the ground. Dead.

Pledgistopheles lowered the freshly used remote control and walked away.

Dr. Cuddles dragged the body away. A cold chill reverberated through Percy's sphincter.

Terminator Rex said, "Anybody else wanna interrupt the test?"

Everyone buried their eyes and heads into their test books.

Percy followed suit, but the last thing on his mind was the test.

The wig still itched. So did the robe. Red bumps multiplying on his arms, begging to be scratched. The chain chafed his neck.

He flipped through the book and didn't know where to begin. *Another electrocution. For being late? Why didn't I see that woman before? And who was she? Kent's replacement? Kinda fucked up to go out like Waffle House hash browns. I don't think I'll be ordering them any time soon. Assuming I make it out of here. Then again, I could use some waffles right about now. Yeah. Waffles. With syrup. That would be tasty.*

Percy felt a glare and turned. Syph waved her pencil at him and stabbed towards the book.

She mouthed, *Write, fucker.*

Percy shrugged and held his palms up and out. Syph sucked her teeth, went stone-faced, buried her face in the test book. Percy slumped in his chair, head in hands, done. Until he heard a familiar whistle.

The Candyman?

He turned and saw Syph, casually writing on her answer sheet. Whistling *The Candyman.*

Trent banged on the wall and roared.

More whistling.

More banging.

More roaring.

Dr. Cuddles ambled in. "The fuck is going on in here?"

Trent stood up. "Somebody's whistling."

"I don't hear shit."

Trent started whistling *The Candyman.*

Dr. Cuddles grinned. "I love that song."

Trent said, "I can't concentrate and listen to whistling at the same time."

Dr. Cuddles sulked. "You can't?"

"No."

Dr. Cuddles clapped his hands for attention. "Everybody stop your tests." They did. "Trent has a problem with whistling. He can't focus. So here's what we're gonna do. Everybody knows *The Candyman?* They did. "I want all a' you to whistle it while you work on your test. Just to help Trent overcome his problem."

Nobody knew what to make of it. Until Syph whistled.

Stranger joined in. As did Percy. Soon everyone, even Bridget, followed *The Candyman* chorus. Everyone but Trent, who sank his head in his folded arms. Dr. Cuddles played conductor.

Percy whistled while looking at the test questions.

And the scales fell from his eyes.

34

TERMINATOR REX HUMMED as he handed out the graded practice tests before exiting with Pledgistopheles. Percy looked over his completed test sections entitled KIDNAPPING, SEARCHES, and CONSPIRACY before shrieking.

"I'll be damned."

He had a perfect score.

"This is crazy. Absolutely crazy."

Stranger gave him a noogie and damn near knocked off Percy's wig. "You signed up for it, killer."

"No, I didn't."

"So you were just minding your business when all of a sudden you called someone to drug your ass and drag you here, right?"

"They do that to you, too?"

"Stop shitting me, motherfucker."

"I swear to God. It's the truth."

"How'd they know you were a lawyer who needed to pass the bar?"

"Beats me. I just woke up in the frat house."

"Goddamn."

"I know. It's crazy."

"You understand what this means? Now I've got..." Stranger's eyes darted. "You? Everything? Shit."

Stranger stormed off.

Percy's robe itched. His scalp pulsated.

Percy took off his wig. Picked at his bumps. Some popped blood. Others popped pus. Probably get infected if he didn't wash his hair.

35

PERCY ROAMED TO A POND in the back, thinking about washing away all of the horror experienced at Pledgistopheles's by taking a bath there. Until he took a whiff of its rancid odor.

The water had different colors because there were oil slicks all over it. Where he didn't find oil, he spied green water. He found a fishing trap with no fish in it, which was good, because Percy was so hungry he'd probably eat whatever monstrosity was in the trap... even if it looked like Blinky, the three-eyed fish from *The Simpsons,* or Seaman, the talking fish with a human face and Leonard Nimoy's voice.

Hell, if it looked like Seaman, he'd have to eat it, just to tell the tale.

Walking along the length of the water, Percy still had no clue where he was. As a Manhattanite, he only ventured off the island when skipping town.

Nevertheless, Percy made his way back inside.

Terminator Rex greeted him with a bag in the chest. Percy opened it and found a wrench, treasure map, one book of matches, and a note he didn't read while Dr. Cuddles did his best Fonz.

"Aaay!"

Percy would not disappoint Dr. Cuddles.

"Ay."

"Da Fonz don't say 'Ay'. Da Fonz says, 'Aaay!'"

Percy tittered, but Dr. Cuddles wouldn't let him off the

hook. "Come on. Like Fonzie."

Percy gave his weakest Fonz ever.

"Aaay."

"Get the fuck outta here."

36

THE TEMPERATURE DROPPED. A shivering Percy wandered the streets, guided by a treasure map with red "X marks the spot." One industrial building after another, abandoned, with names he didn't recognize. A business graveyard. Zombie-free, he hoped. He spied a window with a red "X" matching the building on his map. He took out the wrench, wrapped with a handwritten label which read "TAP ON X."

Burglary. Requires breaking and entering.

Percy had studied the bar enough times to know that a constructive breaking didn't require actually breaking anything. He just needed to force his way in.

Threats count, right? Instead of a front door, a long piece of plywood rested in the frame. Percy moved it. *Forced that aside. Now a threat.* He tripped on his robe. Regained his footing. Looked around. *What if someone's in here? Probably kick my ass if my threat's too mean.* Percy rubbed his chin. *I need a shave. I can feel an ingrown hair festering.* Percy caught himself and stomped. *Focus, fucker. You need to make a threat.*

Percy mugged mean. His eyes darted as he put on his best Jack Nicholson and whispered, "Here's Percy!" No one responded, so Percy exhaled. *Breaking and entering? Check.*

Inside he found a barren pad with a fireplace, an empty bucket of fried chicken, and used Taco Bell wrappers. *Seems like a campout. Maybe a safe joint for one of Pledgistopheles's soldiers hiding from the law? An interrogation room? Tortured by tortillas and the Colonel's Extra Crispy Chicken?* It didn't make sense to Percy, until he saw a half-eaten, petrified biscuit. *I know how they did it. Probably forced someone to eat it. Without gravy.* Percy shuddered, almost forgetting why he was there in the first place.

Focus, fucker.

He rubbed his temples. *Crime time, baby.*

Percy took out the note. *I totally forgot to look at it earlier.* It read, "ASSIGNMENT—BURGLARY/ARSON." He pulled out the matches, which he'd totally forgotten were in the bag. He warmed his hands with his breath, knowing he'd have to burn something other than wallpaper to satisfy the arson requirement.

How could he do that without Pledgistopheles frying his ass?

Maybe this is a setup? I'd start a fire and cops would bust through a fake wall, like DC Mayor Marion Barry. I'd be stuck saying 'Set me up, goddamn' in an infinite loop. Still, even if it wasn't a setup, what about my buddies Monty and Butch? Probably plunger my ass after the fake drugs shtick. Percy's temperature plummeted with every possibility.

First warmth. Next nap. Then I'll figure something out.

Tossing the bucket and wrappers into the fireplace, Percy struck a Pledgistopheles-supplied match, and lit a fire.

Burn, baby, burn.

The fire comforted him. Stress burned away. Sleep overcame him. Fire crackled from the old chicken and taco grease on the refuse. It popped like Jiffy Pop on the stove.

Microwave popcorn for you youngins out there. All toasty and shit.

Percy slept with a smile on his mousy face. Wiggled his toes.

Warmth.

Sparks shot out and hit Percy's shoelaces. By the time Percy woke up, his feet were on fire. He leapt up, screaming. He hiked his robe up to his knees and kicked his shoes off.

They flew in the air like fireballs and ignited the rug and

curtains upon impact.

They engulfed the shack in flames.

His exits?

All blocked.

He clucked the word 'fuck' like a freshly castrated chicken. "Fuck, fuck, fuck, fuck, fuck, fuck, fuck."

His head bobbled. His eyes rapidly darted back and forth.

Until they landed on the red "X" on the window.

Percy took the wrench out of the bag and hurled it at the pane like that dude in the original Apple Macintosh commercial.

The wrench flew. Collided with the wall. Missed the "X" by three feet.

Percy picked up the wrench, summoned Thor, god of thunder, and wielded the wrench as if it was Mjölnir, the enchanted hammer. He smashed it against the window. Cleared the glass with his bag. Got the fuck out of Dodge.

"Fuck me."

Like Orpheus escaping Hades, Percy couldn't look back. Not that there was a hot chick like Eurydice behind him. Just a hot fucking mess he'd left behind. Percy, purveyor of carnage. He liked the sound of it.

He remembered the old Mötley Crüe video where Nikki Sixx lit his pants afire. But the flaming leather pants hadn't set anything else ablaze. So Percy felt totally lied to by the Crüe, and planned to give them a piece of his mind if they ever crossed paths.

With each step away, his emotions surged. He was shoeless and intoxicated by the mayhem.

Percy wheezed heavily from the earlier smoke inhalation. Being out of shape didn't help.

He staggered back to Pledgistopheles's. He wished he had his inhaler. He realized that in spite of everything that occurred that evening, he'd finally done something right.

His eyes gleamed. Chest thrust out. He was the cock of the walk.

A proud, charred Percy strutted to Pledgistopheles and

Dr. Cuddles. "Guys, you wouldn't believe—"

"Sit on it, Fonzie. We heard about the 'fire'. Or should I say 'defective fireplace.'"

Percy slapped his hands against his own cheeks.

"It wasn't the fireplace. It was the Fonz!"

Dr. Cuddles said, "Aaay, calm down, Fonz."

Pledgistopheles looked at Percy sideways. "When'd you decide to burn it down?"

Percy stiffened. "After I broke in. It was cold, so I started a fire."

Pledgistopheles tilted his head away from Percy. "A fire you decided to start after you broke in?"

Percy squeezed his eyes shut. "Right. Breaking and entering plus a crime is burglary."

Dr. Cuddles snapped his fingers at Percy. "Burglary's a crime when you break in with intent to commit a specific crime."

Percy spread his fingers out in a fan against his chest. "Just like I said."

Pledgistopheles bared his teeth. "You intended warmth, motherfucker. The arson's incidental."

Percy's eyes narrowed. "Which means?"

Pledgistopheles' eyebrows lowered and pinched together. "No crime, asshole."

Percy's cheeks burned hotter than his botched arson attempt. His voice cracked. "I failed."

Pledgistopheles's lips curled. "You did worse." He raised the remote at Percy. "Dr. Cuddles?"

Percy looked down at his chain. His mind raced. *This is it. I'm doomed.* He needed to say something. Anything to stop his electrocution execution. Percy opened his mouth.

Nothing came out.

His eyes searched the room for help. Maybe Syph would step in? Maybe Trent?

If they were there.

They weren't.

Percy would die alone.

"I got this, boss." It was Dr. Cuddles, who tossed a shoebox at Percy.

"Open it."

Percy's hands trembled. *A shoebox bomb?* His fingers couldn't work the lid.

Dr. Cuddles said, "Look at him, boss. Just like a birthday boy. All excited to open his pressie." He started singing the birthday song, intensifying Percy's nervousness.

Pledgistopheles snapped his fingers. "Come on, already."

That didn't help either.

Pledgistopheles raised the remote at Percy. "You wanna do it this way instead?"

It was all Percy needed to hear. He opened up the box with one eye closed.

The contents forced both eyes open.

"Slippers?"

Dr. Cuddles rushed Percy. "Try them on."

Percy didn't know if it was some kind of trick. A foot torture? Toxic Dr. Scholls?

Percy grimaced as he slipped in his bare right foot.

"Does it fit?"

Percy nodded. Put the left slipper on his other bare foot. It also fit.

Dr. Cuddles said "Lemme see you walk around in 'em."

Percy feared the worst. A land mine sole that would vaporize him? Perhaps "death after five steps" like *Kill Bill?* Maybe Pledgistopheles was a foot fetishist and the slippers would insulate Percy's feet after getting fried by the remote from hell?

Dr. Cuddles shoved him forward and ran to Pledgistopheles.

Percy swallowed hard. Hiked up his robe in case his slippers burst into flames. Took his first sweaty step.

All shaky.

Pledgistopheles asked, "How does it feel?"

Percy lied. "Good."

Dr. Cuddles' face sank. He turned to Pledgistopheles. "It'll be different once he puts on the second slipper."

Pledgistopheles tapped his foot. "It better."

Percy put on the second slipper.

Dr. Cuddles fidgeted. "How about now?"

Percy squeaked. "Just like the first."

Dr. Cuddles said, "Take ten steps and let me know."

Percy felt the blood pumping through his veins with each step. His scalp bumps pulsated. Dr. Cuddles picked his nails while sucking his inner cheek meat.

The closer Percy got to the tenth step, the heavier his legs felt. His nutsack hairs stood at attention, waiting for the dreaded tenth step.

Percy's foot slowly stepped down.

This was it.

Pledgistopheles said, "That's ten steps, Fonzie."

Nothing. Maybe a malfunction?

Pledgistopheles looked at Percy's feet. "You tried them out. So you tell me and Dr. Cuddles the truth. No bullshit."

Percy nodded.

Pledgistopheles asked, "Are those the most comfortable slippers you've ever worn? I need to know because my mama said, 'Never cheat your feet.'"

Percy grimaced. "My feet?"

Dr. Cuddles said, "You needed new shoes? From the fire?"

Percy cleared his throat. "This is about—"

Pledgistopheles said, "Comfort, motherfucker. You can't be running around doing jobs and studying if your feet hurt."

Dr. Cuddles crouched to Percy's feet. "I think it's too snug." He touched the tip of Percy's slippered foot. "Got enough room?"

Percy wiggled his toes. "Sure."

Dr. Cuddles asked, "And they're not comfy?"

Percy shrugged. "I've worn better."

Dr. Cuddles slapped the ground. "Swear to God, I'm gonna fuck up that douche at Shoetown for selling me this shit."

Pledgistopheles waved at Dr. Cuddles. "They close in ten, so let's skedaddle."

Dr. Cuddles followed him to a hooptie with tinted windows. And drove off.

Percy had lied about the slippers. They felt awesome. Like he'd stepped on the softest pillow ever. Whoever created them was the Willy Wonka of shoes. Shoemaking elves, eat shit. Oompa Loompas were running thangs.

These were the most comfortable pair of slippers he'd ever worn.

Despite all the abuse, all the debasement, he'd die like a prince. He looked down at his chain. Percy now knew they fried for bar failure, but not for mission failure.

At least not yet.

Someone came out of nowhere and snatched Percy. "We don't have much time."

37

"**LET'S GO.**" Stranger tugged Percy towards a port-a-potty.

"Hey, man. I don't roll like that."

Stranger pulled Percy's robe. "Get in here, Percy."

Percy pulled back. "Dude, I'm not joking."

Stranger grabbed more robe. "Neither am I." He started a tug of war with Percy. "In here. Now."

"No."

More tugging.

Stranger opened the door with his free hand and tugged. Percy didn't realize his back was to the potty until it was too late.

Stranger let go and Percy tumbled backwards into the potty.

Stranger jumped in, crowded Percy, shut the door and patted Percy down.

Stranger said, "I'm an undercover cop, tracking this operation for seven years."

"Are you kidding me?"

"I went to law school and failed the bar God knows how many times just for this chance. I thought you were full of shit until Internal Affairs confirmed your story. They're meeting us at my place to put you in protection and take Pledgistopheles down."

"Wait a minute. You're a cop?"

"Keep it down. I got a few things to show you."

"Now?"

Before leaving the potty, Percy pulled the wig over his face to hide his identity. He stumbled and bumbled his blind ass out. After what seemed like hundreds of steps, Percy felt safe enough to lift his wig.

He recognized the neighborhood. The same as Percy's arson assignment.

"Stranger, I don't think this area's safe."

"Don't worry. We've had this safe house for years." Stranger stopped and stared at Percy's feet. "Nice slippers."

It was an abandoned crack house. Or so it seemed. Inside there were photos of Pledgistopheles, Dr. Cuddles, other mob guys, the students, and a flow chart tying together the conspiracy. It looked straight out of every mafia movie Percy had ever seen.

Stranger pointed to different photos. "This area's gone to shit since the factory closed down. The college is garbage and barely keeps the town in the black. Not much happens, since it's a commuter campus. We noticed a spike in criminal activity the weekend before every bar exam. The local cops told us it was frat activity. They didn't know the truth."

"Which is?"

"A diversion. Have people dress in these stupid getups and everyone thinks we're stupid pledges running around town wearing dirty wigs and robes while eating out of dumpsters. It's the perfect cover."

"This is too much."

"You ain't seen the half of it. Wait until my backup gets here."

"I can't take all of this standing up." Percy spied a bathroom. "May I?"

"Number one or number two?"

"Number one, of course. What do you take me for?"

"Then you may."

Percy rushed to the bathroom, closed the door, and stared at the toilet.

He wasn't able to bring himself to use Pledgistopheles's

loo. It was too unsanitary.

But this? It was heaven.

Percy wanted to savor the moment. He gingerly placed the seat down. Tore sheets of toilet paper to cover the seat. Flushed before sitting. Hiked up his robe and descended with care.

As he got down to business, someone knocked at Stranger's front door. Percy heard two familiar voices.

"Told you he'd be here."

"Don't you mean, 'told you he'd be here, sir?' Is that what you mean, rook?"

"Who the hell are you?"

"Your backup."

Percy heard a scuffle.

"The hell is that?"

Percy peeped through the keyhole and spied Monty and Butch beating down Stranger. Percy was so horrified, he wouldn't need an enema for at least a month.

Not soon after the beating, Dr. Cuddles emerged from behind the cops.

"You think we wouldn't find out?"

Stranger's eyelids flapped. His mouth moved like a fish out of water.

"Your boys work for us." Dr. Cuddles pulled out a cellphone and dialed. "Got him here, boss. Fire when ready."

The gold chain around Stranger's neck hummed and shook. He panicked and the chain smoked. Stranger convulsed. Sparks popped from his robe. The white wig on his head turned flush with crimson. Stranger screamed. "My bowels! My bowels! I'm pooping! Please, for the love of God, let me die with dignity!"

Percy heard shitting sounds. Stranger flopped on the ground, butt twerking and twitching.

Dead.

A cop dragged Stranger's shitty carcass away. The other cop put the conspiracy web and photos in a trash can and lit a match.

Dr. Cuddles checked the apartment and realized something was amiss.

"Check the bathroom."

Percy freaked out.

He tried getting up, but he kept stepping on his robe, trapping himself on the seat. He rolled sideways off the potty, but his robe flew up and engulfed his face. Percy wrestled with the robe. Whipping around. Flailing. Finally freeing himself.

He scoped out the bathroom for ways to escape and spied a window. Too tight a fit.

He saw a can of hairspray on the sink and sprayed it on his fingers.

"Slippery."

He sprayed his robe.

Outside the bathroom, Dr. Cuddles's cronies fidgeted with the locked door.

Dr. Cuddles couldn't believe the incompetence.

"What the fuck are you doing?"

Dr. Cuddles broke down the door.

"Goddamn it!"

The bathroom was empty.

*　　*　　*

PERCY RAN FROM Stranger's apartment, puzzling over the evening.

Butch and Monty are working for Pledgistopheles? Or is Dr. Cuddles freelancing on his own? Why'd they shake me down? Maybe to test if I'd rat Pledgistopheles out?

Percy shuddered.

I gotta make it back before they do. If I don't, I'm fucked.

38

WHEN PERCY ARRIVED at Pledgistopheles's frat house, all his fellow captives stood in a makeshift police lineup. Percy didn't know what to do but line up right next to Syph.

Pledgistopheles paced in front of them. "Stranger's not studying with us no more. Anybody got a clue why?"

Trent was happy to help. "Maybe Fonzie could shed some light on the matter."

Percy strained to grin. "I don't know what he's talking about."

Pledgistopheles said, "You got something to say, Fonzie? We ain't making you jump the shark here. You're amongst friends."

Dr. Cuddles arrived in a heap. Pledgistopheles exchanged glances with him.

"Somebody here was with him. Anybody know who?"

Nope.

Dr. Cuddles stood behind Syph, sniffed, stared at Percy. "Fonzie. What were you doing an hour ago?"

Percy scratched his robe. "Studying."

Dr. Cuddles stepped behind him. "Studying?"

Percy felt Dr. Cuddles's eyes checking him out. "Yes."

Dr. Cuddles sniffed him. "You ever work with Stranger?"

"Once."

Pledgistopheles leaned into him. Percy felt hot breath on his neck. "You like him?"

"Not really."

Dr. Cuddles dry-washed his hands. "That's a good thing. Because Stranger was a nut. He didn't seem to like our class. But you're different."

"Right. Different."

Pledgistopheles pushed Dr. Cuddles away from Percy. "Leave him alone, Cuddles. He's tired."

"Sorry, boss."

"And what do you do? You manhandle him, ya mook!" He slapped Dr. Cuddles like a bad dog.

Cuddles cowered like a puppy. "Sorry, boss."

Pledgistopheles tossed Percy a bag. Percy rummaged through it and pulled out a tire iron.

"What am I supposed to do with this?"

"Reading is fundamental, motherfucker."

Percy read the attached note.

"I can't do this."

"Why not?"

"It says armed robbery."

"So what?"

"I can't. I'm sorry. I just can't."

"I understand. You might whack somebody and whacking someone's a big thing, you know."

"That it is."

"Then you shouldn't do it, right?"

"Ummm…"

"Then don't."

"Really?"

"Yup."

"Thanks, Mister Pledgistopheles."

"No problem."

"You sure?"

"Positive."

"I'll just get another bag."

"You do that."

As Percy reached for another bag, Pledgistopheles cracked him on the head. Fortunately, the wig cushioned the blow.

Percy knew better than to gloat. So he pretended it hurt.

"Ow."

Pledgistopheles pointed at Percy. "You listen to me, you piece of shit. You're gonna rob a motherfucker or I kill you. You got me?"

Percy got him, but Pledgistopheles wasn't finished.

"You're gonna go to a party tonight. You're gonna rough up a guy with blue hair who owes me money and you're gonna get my money from the prick. Then you're gonna come back here and give me my money. If I don't see money, I'm gonna commit an aggravated assault on your ass. You got that?" Pledgistopheles got in his face. "On your ass!"

Pledgistopheles and Dr. Cuddles stormed out of the frat house.

Percy tapped a fist against his head.

"Armed robbery? Syph, what am I gonna do?"

Syph stared skyward. Poked the inside of her cheek with her tongue. "I'll do it for you. Just take these."

She handed him some pills.

Percy shook them in his hands like dice. "What's this?"

"Shut the fuck up and take them."

"Where'd you get them?"

"My assignment."

"To do what?"

"If you knew what it was and what those will do to you, you'll have no legal defense, okay?"

"Why are you doing this?"

"Take 'em. Now!"

He did.

"Now here's what we're gonna do, Percy. You're going to go to the party. All fucked up."

"How about you?"

Syph pulled back her sleeves. "I'm gonna put that tire iron to use."

"Thanks, Syph." He staggered back. "Wow, I'm starting to feel the pills. This is strong stuff. Started in my mouth and now is causing my head to tingle." He started jumping up and down like a loon. "I'm high as a kite!"

Percy continued acting the fool as Syph mumbled something about his breath. For sure, his mouth tasted minty. He told himself it was probably a sensory hallucination from the drug.

Percy bumbled out barely able to walk, much less commit a crime. Still, he knew what he had to do.

39

TOOK FOREVER TO GET to the party. Percy stumbled and bumbled the entire way.

"Syph, you know what I don't get?"

"Anything you do get?"

"Good one."

"The fuck you staring at?"

"You. I mean, how'd you end up with a name like Syph?"

"How'd you end up with a name like Percy?"

"It's short for Percival."

"Perci-what?"

"The Knight of the Round Table?"

"King Arthur shit?"

"Yup. Moms was a nerd. How about you?"

"We're not talking about me."

"Oh, come on."

Syph kept walking.

"Please, Syph?"

More walking.

"We got a ways to go, right? And it's just a story. I mean, none of this seems real."

She stopped and turned to him.

"Fine. I'll tell you a story."

*   *   *

ACCORDING TO SYPH, her name derived from Syphilis, a loathsome name culminating from a lingually challenged mother without protection and a promiscuous nurse.

After assisting with the birth, the nurse asked, "Would you like to name your daughter?"

The new mother pondered the question. She knew the gravity of naming. Should she honor her mother? Forge a new path for her child? The possibilities raced through her mind.

Until it came to her.

She smiled and said, "Si, Phyee-liz."

The nurse could barely contain a chuckle. "Yes?"

"Si, Phyee-liz."

The nurse didn't speak Spanish and detested Dominican immigrants whom she blamed for ruining the Bronx. Instead of asking for a second opinion or assuming the woman meant 'Yes, Feliz' or the anglicized 'Yes, Phyllis', she took the answer literally. And ruined the little girl's life by writing down 'Syphilis'.

Syphilis tried calling herself Phyllis or Feliz, but she was stuck with Syphilis throughout elementary and secondary school. Attendance, her free lunch card, and even graduation foiled her name-changing efforts. Once a kid heard the name, that kid wasn't forgetting. And that kid said it as many times as annoying little kids say shit that amuses them. Other kids heard it and spread it. There was no inoculation for her loss of innocence.

Growing up with the name Syphilis put a chip on her shoulder more massive than a boy named 'Sue'. The name eventually became a scarlet letter Syphilis wore proudly, reflecting the slights and humiliations of the immigrant experience. No one facing Syphilis in any ethnic student election stood a chance against her.

Syphilis studied hard at CUNY while holding down two jobs. She eventually shortened her name to 'Syph', to make things easier. Syph didn't know much about law school, but everyone told her she was too smart to be anything but a doctor or lawyer. Syph feared killing a patient, so she opted for law school.

40

"TOTALLY MAKES SENSE, Syph. Totally. But you're smart, so why are you here?"

"The Bar isn't an IQ test."

"I know, but you seem to know everything."

"Compared to your dumb ass."

"No, silly." Percy giggled. "You know the law already, so I don't get why you're here."

Syph stopped. "Doesn't matter."

"I think it does. I mean, you're here, right?"

"We're here."

"Yeah, we're here. But, I mean—"

"Hear that?"

Percy squinted.

"We're here."

She pointed to a converted factory building. Before Percy knew it, Syph went inside. He heard her make a sound that was half-laugh, half-snarl.

It was a Parisian-themed party. Glasses shaped like the Eiffel Tower. A cake with the Arc de Triomphe. Napoleon busts.

A partygoer offered Percy an Eiffel Tower glass. Percy nodded and said, "*Merci.*"

The partygoer offered one to Syph. Syph slapped it away.

A few feet later, Percy offered her a baguette.

She nabbed it from him and beat him in the head with it. "Fuck this French shit."

His wig cushioned the blow. Not that the baguette was hard enough to do any kind of damage. Physically, that was. Percy was emotionally wounded. He loved the French. Their food. Their style. Their *joi de*—something he couldn't pronounce. Especially high on whatever Syph had given him, which made him feel invigorated. He even considered kicking it to the pouty-lipped partygoer with the raspberry beret. After all, she must've liked Prince the same way he did. But he'd have to come up with something more original. Something more—

Syph shoved him forward. She gestured at a blue-haired druggie staggering upstairs.

Syph showed stealthy ninja-like tracking. Graceful, quiet steps covered a lot of ground in seconds. Percy trailed behind her. He stalked the dude with the grace of a wounded water buffalo, stomping and clomping. The dude stumbled into a bathroom.

Syph whispered, "You act as lookout while I handle the business."

Syph grabbed the tire iron from under her robe, went in the bathroom and gingerly closed the door behind her.

After a few seconds of silence, Percy overheard a crash, a few thuds, and a screech.

"Syph?" He didn't know if she needed help. Maybe this drug guy was packing heat. The fuck could Percy do if he was? Should he head back to the garage? Stand his ground? Open the door and—

Syph emerged with the tire iron and scratch as in money, but not a scratch or drop of blood.

Percy looked into the bathroom. Saw toes pointed skyward, attached to scrawny legs in a bathtub. The rest of the body lay behind a shower curtain.

Syph handed Percy the money. On the way out she stopped at the Napoleon bust.

And busted it with the tire iron.

As Percy left the party, he saw someone who looked familiar. Someone he wished Syph had cracked with the tire iron.

Percy rushed out of the party hoping his cover wasn't blown.

41

AT THE FRAT HOUSE, Percy handed Pledgistopheles the money.

"Good job, Fonzie. All you needed was motivation."

A guy and a girl dressed like Percy and his fellow 'pledges' staggered into the frat house. Percy didn't recognize either one.

He wouldn't get the chance. Pledgistopheles got in their faces soon as they entered. "We gave you spots and you fuck 'em up."

Exasperation swept over the pledges' faces.

Anger swept over Pledgistopheles's. "What happened to the guy you were supposed to rough up?"

The new gal wiped her sweaty brow with her robe sleeve. "He was snorting coke, so I offered him Pop Rocks. You know…"

"I don't know shit."

"Pop Rocks and coke are a deadly combination."

"Pop Rocks and Coke the soda, not coke the drug."

"Oh."

The gold chain around her neck hummed, shook, and smoked. She convulsed. Sparks popped from her robe. She flopped on the ground.

Dead.

The new dude feverishly scratched his wig.

"And your guy had a small, pea-sized swelling at the back of his head."

"That was me, Pledgistopheles," the dude replied.

"Do you fly and go 'bzz bzz'?"

"No."

"Right. So you didn't do it. The swelling was caused by a mosquito bite and had jack shit to do with to his death."

"But I hit him. I swear to God I hit him."

Pledgistopheles tapped the dude's wig. "How are we supposed to know that?"

"You saw me do it."

"What the fuck?" Pledgistopheles groaned. "You think we got cameras in those chains?"

"I had the brass knuckles, with the intent to kill. I saw the guy. I whacked him in the head. At least give me attempted murder. I mean, look at these chicken wings." He pulled back his robe and revealed bony arms with hardly a hint of meat or muscle.

"You didn't do the job." Pledgistopheles raised the remote at him. The dude lunged and grasped Pledgistopheles's trigger finger.

Percy gnawed the neck of his robe like a dog on a chew toy.

Pledgistopheles looked down at the dude's hands. Eyes widened. The dude released Pledgistopheles's finger as soon as he touched it and jumped back, hands raised, lips quivering.

"Sorry, sir."

Pledgistopheles raised the remote. "Apology acc—"

"Wait!" The dude flapped his hands in the air. "Wait, please. The mosquito bite? That was me. And that has to count for something, right? I mean, think about it."

Percy's toe hairs raised in anticipation of the electrocution. He couldn't bear to look.

Neither could Pledgistopheles. He lowered the remote.

The dude exhaled. "Good. Good. Look, I just got here and I'm doing my best. Under the circumstances."

Pledgistopheles gritted. "You know, you're right. We fucked up." He put a snug arm around the pledge. "I apologize. Next time we give you a job, you'll get the appropriate tools, okay? Just don't go around telling folks we didn't give you the right materials for study. It could cost our rep. And that, my friend, is hard to come by." He patted the student on the back and walked away.

The pledge nodded, turned to Percy and winked.

Pledgistopheles turned to him. "I forgot something."

The pledge said, "Yeah?"

"Does the bar exam have an appeals process?"

"Appeals?"

"You know, for not getting credit for a right answer graded wrong?"

"I don't know."

"I do." Pledgistopheles raised the remote control at him. Aimed and pressed a button with a fat finger.

The gold chain around the pledge's neck hummed and shook. The student panicked and the chain smoked. He convulsed. Sparks popped from his robe. The white wig on his head turned flush with crimson. Piss streamed from his robe and he flopped on the ground.

Dead.

Pledgistopheles said, "Anybody else got a problem with their study materials?"

42

OUTSIDE, TRENT STARED at the frat house. "We have to go to the cops. Now."

Syph cackled. "And tell them what?"

Percy made sure the coast was clear before whispering. "Pledgistopheles has cops on his payroll."

Trent whiffed. "As if."

Percy said, "I saw them kill Stranger."

Syph blinked rapidly. "You what?"

"Cuddles called Pledgistopheles on the phone, who in turn electrocuted Stranger remotely."

"You're full of shit." Trent walked away. "See you on *COPS*."

Percy grabbed him. "If you rat on us, we're dead."

Trent elbowed him away. "Get the fuck off me."

"He's not going to the cops." Syph chortled. "He's gonna call his daddy."

"At least I know who my daddy is."

She leapt in his face, fist cocked. She smiled. "You know what? Go to the cops. Get your ass beat down."

Trent made his way down the street. Percy followed.

"Trent, if you finish this course and pass the bar, no one can ever take it away from you. You can be your own man."

The notion stopped Trent in his tracks. Syph soldiered on.

"Fuck him, Percy. I've already wasted too much of my life helping his spoiled ass out. I got a job to do."

She picked up a bag and rolled out.

Trent leered at his chain, his robe. He took off his wig. Nodded. Nabbed a bag. Stared at it. "My own man." He walked away, upright, chest forward, shoulders back.

Percy hunched forward, scratched his head and grabbed a bag. This time he read the note before going anywhere. "FOLLOW BRIDGET, MICHELLE." He didn't know a Michelle and figured it was the wrong bag. Maybe belonged to the dead pledge replacement. He considered telling Pledgistopheles. Thought against it once he set eyes on his crotchety ass. *Maybe it's a rib*. Percy kept the note as evidence and spied Bridget in the distance.

She tottered down the street, twisting her dreads. Percy pursued her for a while until she turned around.

"Why are you following me?"

Percy showed her the note.

Her face caved in on itself. "Your name is Michelle?"

"No, but whoever she is, I figured I have her bag, so I might as well, you know?"

"Right."

Bridget's hands trembled.

Percy said. "You okay?"

"I'm under a lot of stress. I'm in some frat house from hell located who knows where. Dressed like a clown. People dying. And for what? I shouldn't even be here. But I am, and I don't even have a clue what constitutes attempt."

Percy understood her confusion, her frustration. At least he thought he did.

He was clueless.

Syph drove by in a hooptie. "Get the fuck in."

43

BRIDGET RODE IN THE BACK seat with Percy, who scoped the ride.

"They give you this?"

Syph looked at him in the rear view. "I stole this."

A glimmer of hope shone in Bridget's eyes. "Maybe we can escape."

"Only thing we're escaping is bar failure." She tossed something at Bridget. "Take this."

Bridget bumbled it. "An Uzi?"

"A toy. You pull the trigger, it makes a noise."

"What if someone dies of a heart attack?"

"We'll pick someone young and healthy. Like him." Syph pointed at an unsupervised five-year-old on the corner.

Bridget said, "How about I use my finger? It's just like a gun." Sure enough, Bridget made a finger gun. "Pow!"

Syph dragged her hands through her wig hairs, more roughly each time Bridget 'shot' someone with a finger gun. Powder puffed each time.

Percy coughed and rocked slightly. He needed to step in before Syph lost her shit. "Bridget, just use the gun."

"I am," she replied as she aimed and fired at Percy.

Percy nudged her finger gun down. "Bridget, just do it. Please?"

"Fine." Bridget slumped in her seat and took the Uzi. "But I'm not shooting at little boys."

Syph blew out a breath that rattled her lips. "Yeah. You

151

might miss."

Percy spotted new targets. "How about them?" It was a group of taxi drivers.

Bridget sucked her molars. Percy channeled his inner guru.

"Overpriced fares. Intentionally going the wrong way. Almost flattening you in the crosswalk while they're running a red light, just to get an extra fifty cents?"

"They're just trying to follow the American Dream," Bridget retorted. "Plus, haven't they suffered enough backlash from 9/11?"

"True. How about them?" It was a group of teenagers. "Loud, obnoxious, rude. Always bitching about their parents. Taking up three seats in the subway so they can feel each other up." He shouted at a teen couple making out, "Save your allowance for a hotel!"

Bridget lifted her chin. "But they might have guns."

"Good call."

Percy pointed. "How about them?" It was a group of drunken construction workers staggering out of a bar. "Ever walk by a construction site during lunchtime and—"

Bridget squeezed the trigger. Crimson erupted on the jittering workers.

Bridget stopped shooting.

"Holy shit!"

Syph smiled. "I guess they weren't blanks after all."

The workers lurched up, growling.

Bridget grabbed Percy. "Zombies!"

Percy pointed at them. "Shoot the heads!"

Tremors shook Bridget's hands and fingers.

Percy grabbed Bridget's hands. Wrapped them around the gun. "Shoot the heads, Bridget."

Bridget gawked at Percy. She took three attempts to swallow. She raised the Uzi with her eyes as wide as a kewpie doll's. Busted shots. It took five seconds to empty the entire fifty-round magazine. Only five seemed to hit. To no avail.

Bridget said, "They must be super-zombies. It has begun. The gates of hell are full. The dead are walking the earth!"

As they drove off, Syph cackled.

Bridget looked all around. Especially behind. "What's so funny?"

Syph turned and pointed. "You got punk'd!"

"What?"

"Red paintball pellets, Bridget. Good thing we weren't studying bestiality. Probably wouldn't make it past the pet store."

Percy sank in his seat. Bridget slapped her thighs so hard she hurt herself. "Of all the... I lost ten years of my life back there."

Syph said, "You'll lose twenty if you fail the bar again."

"You don't know anything about me."

Syph chortled. "I know you're all butthurt for playing paintball with a bunch of bastards."

Percy said, "Who are you calling a bastard?"

Syph ignored him. "All butthurt. And ungrateful."

Bridget said, "Ungrateful? For what?"

Syph snickered. "She says 'for what'. For keeping your ass alive."

"Scaring me half to death? Lying to me about the blanks?"

"I gotta run every detail by you?"

"You said they were blanks."

"I misspoke."

"You said I was punk'd. You misspeak then, too?"

"I'm not gonna argue semantics with you."

"Semantics?" Bridget nearly stood up in her seat.

"You better sit your ass down and buckle up."

"I don't wanna sit down."

"Fine." Syph pumped the brakes, causing Bridget's head to hit the car ceiling. Wig powder flew everywhere. Enveloping the car interior.

Percy cleared his throat of powder. "Bridget, buckle up."

Bridget held her ground. Figuratively speaking, since her head repeatedly slammed against the roof.

Percy leaned into Syph's seat. "Please stop doing that."

"Doing what?"

"Giving her brain damage."

"Oh boo-hoo, Papa Smurf."

Bridget said, "My brain's fine. Can't say the same for hers."

Syph said, "Don't make me stop this car."

Bridget raised the Uzi. "We're committing crimes here. And for what? To pass the bar?"

Percy said, "They're not crimes, remember? We're eliminating one element to make it perfectly legal. There's no legal liability."

"What about moral liability?"

Syph played the world's tiniest violin.

Percy said, "Bridget, she's just trying to help you. You said you couldn't focus, so she's giving you a taste—"

"A taste? I'm allergic."

Syph said, "We're not doing anything illegal. We're just studying. That's all."

Percy reverted to being a kid, trapped in the car while his parents argued, praying for an end to the ride. They would've arrived if the driver wasn't caught up arguing some bullshit. There was less speed, but more braking. Syph stretched out the ride to score debate points. "Not everything we think is wrong is illegal, nor is everything we think is right legal."

Bridget's neck bent forward. "What's your problem?"

Syph's teeth clenched. "I want to be a lawyer, okay? I took the LSAT, went to law school, and graduated. I just need to pass, and I'm doing what it takes, because I'm gonna be a lawyer, goddamn it."

"Nobody does what we're doing to be a lawyer. Ever think about that?"

"Maybe you're just not meant to be a lawyer. Ever think about that?"

"But—"

"There is no but."

"There is—"

"Do you want to pass?"

"What kind of question is—"

"Do. You. Want. To. Pass?"

"Of course I want to pass."

"Then grow some vagiones."

"Va what?"

"Don't be a victim. Ask yourself how badly you want it. And if you want it badly? Don't just take it by the balls. Rip those fuckers off and stomp the shit out of them. That's all you gotta do instead of sitting back there looking stupid."

Bridget sank deeper in her seat, mouth pinched, eyes narrowed at Percy. He could feel her hatred. Hatred for telling her everything would be okay. That Syph was harmless. He looked at Syph. She hated him, too. Percy closed his eyes and prayed for the ride from hell to end with his wits and life intact.

44

OUTSIDE PLEDGISTOPHELES'S frat house, Dr. Cuddles passed out graded test books.

Percy's improvement continued, especially with topics involving intent, conspiracy, and criminal procedure. Syph displayed her book like a kindergarten teacher at story time. Her hands swept over every page in an exaggerated, open-palm, underhanded manner. Her finger pointed at each correct check, her lips barely contained the world's widest smug grin.

She strolled to Bridget and grabbed her own hoo-hah like Madonna in the *Vogue* video. "Vagiones."

Bridget grimaced at the chicken scratch on her own test book that read: 'HABLAS USTED INGLAIS, SHIT FOR BRAINS?'

Syph worked it like a supermodel to a bag. "Sashay, shante." She wiggled her hips and left.

Bridget walked away, scouring through her study materials.

"A crime involves a voluntary physical act, *actus reus*, together with a guilty mind, *mens rea*, which when taken together must violate a penal statute."

She took out a book entitled "PRACTICE EXAMS" and answered a few questions. She checked her choices. "All wrong."

Her chin trembled, eyes vacant.

Percy wanted to help. He didn't know if a hug would be appropriate or just plain creepy. Same with a back or shoulder rub. So he did the safest thing.

He bit his lip, walked over to her...

... and nodded.

Bridget didn't look at him. So he kept biting his lip and nodding.

Still no response, so he added a, "Yep."

She heard him. "You agree?"

"Yep."

"Then maybe I'm just not meant to be a lawyer."

"I wasn't agreeing to that."

"Then why are you nodding your head?"

"I just—well, look, it's tough, but what choice do we have, you know? Either we do these jobs or we die."

Bridget clutched her ears and rattled her head.

Percy's words of comfort? More like words of doom.

He needed to help. He picked up a study guide. "Let's go with the basics, okay? The four major criminal mental elements, *mens rea*, are CRIB. C for criminal negligence, R for recklessness, I for intent and B for?" He pointed at her like a school teacher. "For?"

Bridget shrugged her shoulders.

Percy said, "You know it."

"Bestiality?"

"Say what?"

Bridget punched her thigh. "It's Syph. Her words. I can't get them out of my head."

"Don't focus on the words. Focus on the actions. What we're doing."

"The crimes?"

"Yes, I mean, no. The actions. Become one with the—"

"The crimes?"

"They're not crimes, we're just pretending. Like actors."

"Actors?"

"Exactly. Actors. You just need to get into the mind of the character."

"Actors."

"Yeah, I mean, we're here doing this, but we're not here

doing this. You know what I mean?"

Bridget tugged at her wig.

Percy said, "Be one with the role."

"What role?"

"You're playing a ingénue."

"En-what?"

"An impressionable young woman. Kidnapped from her home. Forced to break the law. You survive by breaking minor laws."

"First of all, that's me. Not some character. Second, I don't break the law."

"Do you cross the street only when the white man lights up?"

"No, but—"

"Then you're jaywalking. Breaking the law."

"Not really."

"Not really?"

"Never got a ticket."

"So you only break the law when you get caught?"

"This is totally different."

"Look around, Bridget. You think we're breaking the law? We aren't. They are."

They walked so far, they ended up in the downtown area. Surrounded by day-to-day illegality on the street—jaywalking, disturbing the peace, littering, and exposed butt cracks.

Bridget pointed. "What about him?"

It was Trent.

Strolling by an outdoor restaurant. Leering at tips left on empty tables. Trent nabbed the tip money and muttered, "Theft, not larceny." He turned around and put the money back, chanting, "Not theft, not larceny." A few feet away, a man held a pizza slice inches from his mouth. Trent leapt at him and took a bite. "Larceny, not theft." The guy mistook him for a crackhead and tossed the rest of the bitten slice away.

Trent approached Bridget and Percy, grinning, pizza sauce dripping from his mouth.

"It works. Being my own man. Owning this. It really works, just like Syph said. Physically. Legally. It's all coming together."

Trent spied something down the street. "Wait here." He strolled into a dime store. *What was Trent doing inside? Loitering? Robbery? Taking a dump in Aisle Five?* Percy needed to know. Soon as he started to enter, Trent exited.

"Trent, what were you doing in there?"

Trent ran down the block. Percy didn't want to follow, but he had to. By the time he reached him, Trent had shaken down a hooker and taken her money.

Trent wagged a finger. "Don't let me see you on these streets again."

The hooker ran away.

Percy stiffened. "What was that about?"

Trent flashed a toy police badge. "Criminal fraud. Menacing. Unlawful detainment."

"You're gonna keep the money?"

Trent walked into a bodega and bought a six-pack of beer.

Percy rubbed at his forehead. "We're drinking?"

Trent left the bodega, crossed the street and gave the beer to a teenager. "Contributing to the delinquency of a minor."

Trent whipped out a note, dropping soon as he read it. "I still need to do something." He rushed to a parking lot.

Bridget said, "Should we follow him?"

Percy picked up the note. "Seems vanilla enough. Sure."

45

PERCY SLAPPED AT a note. "Trent, this says 'steal a car', not 'hit and run'."

Trent fixated on driving. "I'm just showing some initiative."

Bridget scratched her wig.

Something bellowed outside.

"The hell was that?"

On the sidewalk, a drunk hobo clutched his leg, shaking. Trent stopped the car and got out.

"Percy, help me put him in the car. Bridge'll drive while we take care of him."

Percy leered at the man. "You should be able to handle it by yourself. I mean he's pretty frail-looking. And old. Droopy, skin all hanging—"

"Percy."

"Okay." He gave the codger a once-over. "You don't see any open wounds, do you?"

"Percy!"

"Okay." Percy pulled his robe over his hand, trying to avoid pressing flesh. He grimaced. "Everything fine, sir?"

The man puked on the car floor.

Bridget treated the geezer like he was a sick puppy. Tenderly. Lovingly. She said, "I'll help with him."

Percy's skin flushed as he took the keys from Bridget.

"You might want to drive slowly, Percy."

Percy drove off with Bridget and Trent tending to the old

man in the back seat.

Percy, with eyes on the road, asked the man, "How do you feel?"

Before the guy answered, Percy heard the door open. He turned to see the guy tumbling out of the moving car.

Percy did a double-take. "What the fuck happened?"

Bridget exchanged a knowing glance with Trent. "He fell out."

Percy stopped the car, got out and ambled toward the old man. "We'll take him to the hospital."

Trent jumped out of the car and grabbed Percy. "'We' are not taking him anywhere."

Percy shook him off. "We owe—"

Trent sneered. "'We' do not owe him a goddamn thing."

"What about the Good Samaritan rule?"

Trent twisted his mouth. "He's closer to the hospital than he was a few—"

Percy pointed at their starting point. "I drove three feet."

Trent grinned. "Then there's no legal obligation to drive any further."

Percy gawked. "You've got to be shitting me. Right, Bridget?"

Bridget thumbed through her practice book. "Trent's right. There's no duty to drive any further."

Trent mugged. "Exactly. This, this is how you pass the bar."

Bridget winced. "Can't we take him to the hospital?"

Trent turned to her. "We take him to the hospital and we're toast." He jangled her chain. "Remember?"

Percy put a hand on Trent's shoulder. "Not if we drop him off by the curb. It's the right thing to do."

Trent smacked it off. "Living. That's the right thing to do. Besides, it's not like he'll die."

Percy shook the car keys at Trent. "You don't know that."

Trent snatched the keys from him. "I'm finally kicking legal ass and you want to waste my study time on ethical responsibility?"

Percy nabbed the keys back. "It's not wasted time."

Trent reclaimed the keys. "It's not on the bar."

Percy took the keys from Trent. "We leave him and he's gonna tell."

Trent grabbed the keys from Percy. "Tell who? He was picked up by a gaggle of judges? Nobody'll believe him."

"Don't be so sure." Percy reached for the keys. And missed.

Trent teasingly shook the keys. "He's a drunk bum. He's probably not even really hurt."

Percy smacked the keys out of Trent's hands. "You want to take that risk?"

Trent replied, "Better than getting caught on hospital cam by the cops. Or someone driving by who sees a bum in the backseat."

Percy looked at him sideways. "You never intended to help him when he fell out."

"He didn't fall out." Trent jogged away.

Percy followed. "You pushed him? Out of a moving car?"

Trent turned. "I didn't push shit." He kept trucking.

Percy scratched his wig. "Then how did he—" He turned to Bridge.

She was gone.

So was the car.

46

PLEDGISTOPHELES WADDLED IN. "This is your last job."

Dr. Cuddles handed a bag to the remaining students.

Percy saw Trent. "What about Bridget?"

Cuddles said, "Open your bags."

They did.

"Like what you see?"

Each of them pulled out Tasers and baseball bats.

Percy rummaged through the bag. "Where's the job?"

Pledgistopheles said, "Felony murder, motherfuckers."

Percy clucked. "But that's an unintended homicide—"

"Committed while engaged in a felony."

Percy said, "How can we intend to commit an unintended homicide?"

"That's up to you guys."

"But—"

"No buts, but yours are on the line."

"What about our necklaces?"

"After the job, you come back here and we'll take them off. *Arrivederci.*"

Pledgistopheles left with a kiss-blowing Dr. Cuddles.

Trent blurted out, "Statutory rape."

Percy stepped back. "Statutory rape?"

Trent got all Tony Robbins. "It's just accommodating a teenager who's down for dicking. After I fuck her, Syph will get her father. He'll charge me and you'll Taser him to death."

Percy said, "Why is it me and why is it rape?"

Trent replied, "It's just sex with a fifteen-year-old."

"Do you hear what you're saying, Trent?"

"As long as there's grass on the field, we can play ball."

"Grass on the field?" Percy shook his head. "Not doing it."

"Then you pick the crime where someone ends up in a casket so we can pass the bar."

"You've lost your mind."

Trent's eyes sparkled. "How about this? I have an uncle on the verge of death. He wants an assisted suicide, but my parents won't... indulge him. We steal a car, break in, and pull a Kevorkian."

Syph nodded. "I like it."

Percy didn't. "This is crazy. What if someone's home?"

Trent said, "I'll call his nurse and give her the night off."

Percy said, "You know what? I don't think this is worth it anymore."

Syph slapped his back. "Come on, Percy. It's a great idea."

Percy adjusted his wig. "This is murder we're talking about."

Syph looked at him askance. "So was beating that guy at the house party."

"Beating, not killing. Plus, I was drugged."

"Here." She tried handing two white pills to him.

Percy waved her away. "I'm not taking drugs again."

Trent nabbed them from Syph, popped them in his mouth and recoiled. "These are breath mints."

Percy scrunched up his face. "Say what?"

Trent blew in his face.

Percy rubbed his chin. "You sure they aren't mint-flavored drugs?"

Syph sucked her teeth. "They're mint-flavored breath mints, motherfucker. You didn't have a problem with being a part of a killing then, so you can do this now."

Percy started out. "Forget this. I'm leaving."

Before Percy took another step, Syph pulled a Taser on

him.

"Trent," Percy whined, "help me out here."

Trent put his baseball bat to Percy's head and said, "The tribe has spoken."

Percy raised his hands skyward. "Can I at least get some of those breath mints?"

47

THEY DROVE TO A palatial estate a few miles away from the frat house.

After scoping the exterior, Trent took out a wire and started working on the front door lock.

Syph tapped his wig. "I see an open window."

Trent shrugged. "It'll just take me a moment."

Percy yelped. "Are you kidding me?"

Syph walked to the window. "Just come through the window, dumbass."

Trent waved her away.

Syph threw up the finger. "Fine. We'll do the job without you."

"Syph," Percy whispered, "why don't I keep watch out here?"

"You wait outside while he fiddles with the lock?"

"Yes."

"So you can help him with the cops after he wakes up the neighborhood?"

"He's picking the lock."

"And when that doesn't work, he's gonna break open a window."

"Trent's not gonna—Hey, Trent, if this doesn't work, you gonna break a window open?"

Trent replied, "You think I'm stupid?"

"See, Syph?"

Trent laughed and gestured at his bag. "I have a mini torch

to melt the door handle."

Percy stared at Trent. "You're joking, right?"

"Goddamn it, Percy. Keep on interrupting me and I'll throw you through a fucking window."

Percy made his way through the window Syph opened and fell in. Face first.

Percy dusted himself off. He looked around and felt like he was in an off-site storage facility for the Met. There were loads of paintings, antiquities, and things he couldn't pronounce.

"Percy, get over here."

It was Syph.

"Look at this stuff, Syph. Isn't it amazing? I mean check out this Picasso."

"That's a Matisse. Just come on and help me."

He followed Syph to a room. In the corner lay a drooling old man, on the verge of death, attached to a respirator in bed.

Percy scrutinized the geezer's grill. He looked really familiar. "I've seen this guy somewhere before."

"You're just tired."

Percy squinted and leaned closer to him. "No, I'm positive. I've seen him somewhere before. "

"Trent's face. That's where you've seen him."

"He doesn't look like Trent."

"Maybe Trent's adopted."

"Then why does he look so familiar? I don't forget a face. Maybe in the movie—"

"Maybe on *America's Most Wanted?*"

"Wouldn't that be a hoot?" Percy laughed so hard, he almost knocked over a vase.

"Sorry, Syph."

"We have to be quiet if we want to do this."

A window in the hallway crashed open.

Syph wagged her finger. "Told you he'd break the window."

It was Trent.

"Fucking torch didn't work. But look what I found."

A pair of guns. He handed one to Syph.

The elderly man awakened, disoriented. "Is that you, Junior?"

Trent said, "It's me, Uncle. Trent."

"Right. Trent. My nephew."

"Since you're my uncle."

"Right. Uncle." He twiddled his thumbs. "Who are these people? And why are they here?"

"Oh. Meet Syph."

She waved. "Hi."

"And Percy."

Percy nodded. "Hey."

Trent smiled at his uncle. Placed a loving hand on his shoulder. "We're here to kill you."

Percy couldn't believe it.

Neither could the old man. He fist-pumped. "Hallelujah!"

Trent rushed to the respirator and fidgeted with it. "How do I turn this thing off?"

Syph dusted a vase of fresh-cut flowers on a doily atop a grand piano.

Sweat gushed from Percy. "Let me hold all of the guns while you and Syph find out."

Syph pushed him aside. "I'll take the guns, Trent."

"Sure."

He gave her the guns and tussled with the respirator, much to the old man's chagrin.

"Goddamn it, just pull the fucking plug, Trent!"

"Which one?" It was a tangled mess of plugs.

Gramps grimaced. "How the fuck am I supposed to know?"

Syph roamed the room. "Percy, you ever see the movie *Back to School*?"

"Nope."

"Rodney Dangerfield buys his way into college and hires a staff to do his tests and papers. He offers to hook up his son, who refuses help because he wants to make it on his own."

Percy beamed. "Kinda sounds like you, Trent. You know, wanting to make it on your own."

Syph aimed her gun at an oblivious Trent.

The old man loved it. "That'll work too." He pointed at himself. "Right here, darling, after you're done with my nephew."

Percy couldn't believe his eyes.

"What are you doing?"

"Percy, people look at a woman like me and see affirmative action, but what about Trent's affirmative actions?"

Trent turned around and faced the gun.

She continued. "In law school, your daddy's doctor made up some bullshit so all your tests were take-home."

Trent grimaced. "He did?"

Syph said, "Tests you'd fax to your daddy's firm. Where I worked on them and made you top of your class. And what did you do in return? You made me fail the bar."

Percy said, "He did?"

"Why the fuck did you spend your final year of school in Paris, Trent? I had to stop studying for the bar, learn French law, and do your fucking exams. I used to like the French. But since then? I hate frogs. I hate their French law. I hate their French skin. I hate French fries. I hate Gerard Dépardieu's big French nose. I hate Haitians because they speak French. Most of all? I fucking hate *Amélie*."

Percy scratched his head. "What does Trent have to do with France?"

Syph's eyes bored into Trent. "I failed the exam, your daddy panicked, then fired my ass. I anonymously sent him information about Pledgistopheles's class and waited. Waited for the time when he had no choice but to sign you up. Waited to see that twenty grand transfer, since I still had access to his bank accounts. Now I get to study for the bar, waste your ass, and get away with it."

Percy stood dumbstruck. He didn't really understand what was going on. Until it came to him. "The party."

Trent said, "Party?"

Percy bugged out. "That's why you didn't want the baguette, Syph."

Trent said, "Baguette?"

Percy scratched his chin. "We went to a French party. Syph beat me with a baguette."

Syph nodded. "Finally figured it out, Inspector Gadget?"

Trent snickered. "Inspector Clouseau would be more apropos. Since he's French and all."

Syph gritted. "Oh, you wanna make some jokes, now? Here's one for you. Hop like Pepe LePew."

Trent wasn't snickering any more. "Excuse me?"

Syph pointed the gun at him. "You heard me. Hop like Pepe LePew chasing a cat."

"I can't."

"The fuck not?"

"There's no cat."

"A method actor. OK, Dustin Hoffman." She turned to Percy. "You play the cat."

"Excuse me?"

She turned to him. "Run like a cat so Pepe can chase you."

"I don't know what you—"

She raised the gun at him and Percy started running in a circle. "Now hop, Pepe."

Sure enough, Trent started hopping after Percy.

Syph snickered. "Exactly. Just like that. Harass the fuck out of that cat, Pepe."

Trent's uncle applauded. "Oh shit."

Sure enough, Trent harassed Percy Pepe LePew style, hopping towards his prey.

Syph loved every second of it, bent over laughing. Until Trent hopped his ass right on top of her, rumbling for the guns.

Percy closed his eyes.

BLAM.

The guns went off.

Trent's uncle aped Porky Pig, "Th-th-that's all folks."

Percy stared at them as Trent's father sang the Looney Tunes theme.

"Percy?" It was Syph.

Trent's uncle was in the moment. "Yes. Feel it, baby! Go to the light!"

She moaned. "I'm sorry… please…"

Percy didn't know what to do. Trent's uncle had an idea.

"Does she have any bullets left, Percy?"

Percy came to his senses and rushed to help her.

Trent's uncle stewed. "Percy, I asked you a question."

Percy took Syph's hand. "I'll call a doctor."

Trent's uncle sucked his teeth. "Fuck the doctor. I'm next!"

Syph coughed. "No doctors. I'm dying but… don't let this be in vain. You go to Pledgistopheles… take test… pass? You pass…"

"Help me," the uncle whined. "Put me out of my misery."

"No… help yourself, Percy… pass." Syph reached into her pocket. "Here… this… take…"

Percy went to her. She put something in his hand. It was a locket.

She said, "Remember… everything…"

"I'll try."

"No. You do… there is no try…"

Her eyes closed.

Trent's uncle beamed with hope.

"The reaper. He's here. Come on, Percy. Don't keep him waiting. Be a man. Me next."

Percy was too distraught to care. He gathered himself and started to leave, much to the chagrin of Trent's uncle.

"Where are you going? Hey, goddamn it!"

It was too late. Percy left the building.

"Get your ass back in here! I'm still breathing, motherfucker! It'll only take a minute. Hey! Aw, hell."

48

A BLOODY PERCY DROVE back to the frat house.

Pledgistopheles stood outside with Dr. Cuddles, remote raised and pointed at Percy.

"Show us your hands."

Percy extended his shaky arms, palms open and facing front.

Dr. Cuddles rushed him. Pulled a stop-and-frisk. Percy's body ached during the patdown.

Pledgistopheles said, "He clear?"

Dr. Cuddles flashed a Fonzie thumbs-up.

Pledgistopheles still pointed the remote at Percy. "Any last words?"

Percy blinked rapidly. "Last words?"

Dr. Cuddles said, "You heard him."

Percy slightly shook his head. "I could've left. But didn't. Since I completed the job. Felony murder, right?"

Pledgistopheles stood, stone-faced, remote still raised.

Dr. Cuddles said, "Who'd you kill?"

Percy replied, "Nobody."

Dr. Cuddles sneered. "Nobody?"

Percy sighed. "Nobody."

Dr. Cuddles snickered. "Nobody." He turned to Pledgistopheles. "And he said he completed the job. Without killing nobody."

Percy's muscles tightened. "I didn't have to kill anyone."

Dr. Cuddles said, "Why the fuck not?"

Percy, hands on hips, breathed deeply. "Syph. She murdered Trent and I was Syph's partner to the felony burglary. She raised a loaded gun. At Trent. With the intent to murder him."

Dr. Cuddles squinted. "Who murdered Syph?"

Percy got his second wind. "Nobody."

Dr. Cuddles razzed. "She commit suicide?"

Percy shifted his weight to his other foot. "Trent shot her."

Dr. Cuddles forced a smile. "I thought you said—"

Percy rubbed his brow. "You said murder. Trent didn't murder Syph. He shot her in self-defense, okay? I'm still legally responsible because defenses don't attach to co-conspirators to felony murder. Just crimes. Kaypiece?"

Pledgistopheles and Dr. Cuddles exchanged incredulous glances. Dr. Cuddles backed away.

Pledgistopheles lowered his remote and went inside.

Percy exhaled. "It's over?"

Dr. Cuddles whipped out a handgun and raised it at Percy. "Inside, Fonzie."

49

INSIDE THE FRAT HOUSE, Pledgistopheles raised the remote at Percy. "Before we proceed, Fonzie, you got know this is gonna hurt me more than it'll hurt you."

Dr. Cuddles wrapped an unwelcome arm around Percy. "He ain't lying. He hates this part."

Beads of sweat erupted on Percy's forehead, dripping underneath his wig. "You don't have to do this."

Pledgistopheles bit his lip. "I do, Fonzie. We had an agreement. Now close your eyes. This might sting a bit."

Percy clasped his hands together. "You don't have to do this."

Tears welled up in Dr. Cuddles' closing eyes. "I can't look."

"Me neither." Pledgistopheles closed his eyes too, the remote still pointed at Percy.

Percy's mouth opened, but nothing came out.

Pledgistopheles pressed the button.

Percy felt a shock around his neck. A small, static-electricity kind of shock.

And his chain fell off.

Pledgistopheles opened an eye. "It worked?"

Dr. Cuddles opened both eyes. "It worked!"

The two jumped up and down like a high-school cheerleading squad.

"It worked!"

Percy stood, puzzled.

"It worked?"

Pledgistopheles pressed another button and the chain burst into flames. "Wrong button." He pressed another and confetti shot out from the walls while a banner which read "YOU DID IT!" dropped from the ceiling. *Pomp and Circumstance* played on unseen speakers.

It reminded Percy of his high-school graduation.

"Good job, kid." Pledgistopheles patted Percy's head. "Top of your class."

Percy said, "I'm the only one left."

"Be proud."

"But I haven't passed the bar yet."

"Don't be all negative and shit."

"It could happen. I could fail. Then what you gonna do? Come after me for ruining your one hundred percent guarantee?"

"We cross that bridge when we get to it. First you take the bar tomorrow and—"

He noticed a bloody locket in Percy's hand.

"What's that?"

"Syph."

"Syph? She gave this to you?" He looked at Dr. Cuddles, head tilted as if he was mentally weighing it. "Bless her heart. Fonzie, don't let all of this be in vain. She died for you."

Percy stared at the ground. "Don't say that."

"No. You listen. She died for you. If you fail, she died for nothing and you ain't shit. You hear me? You look at that locket and remember all we tried to teach you. You have an opportunity here. Don't fuck it up."

"So I sleep here until the bar?"

"What do I look like I'm running here? A fucking Hilton?"

"I'd like to be fucking Hilton." Dr. Cuddles giggled.

Percy said, "Then what do I do?"

Pledgistopheles blanched his face. "Go the fuck back home, you retard. You gotta get rested up."

"Okay."

175

Percy staggered out. And came back.

"How do I get home from here?"

Dr. Cuddles said, "Terminator Rex'll drive you."

Percy turned to leave.

Pledgistopheles said, "That's how you leave us, Fonzie? As a ingrate?"

"What?"

"Come here."

Percy obeyed.

Pledgistopheles said, "No thanks, Fonzie?"

Percy extended his hand. "Thanks, Pledgistopheles."

"The fuck is that?"

"A hand of thanks and friendship."

"Men don't shake. Men hug."

Pledgistopheles engulfed him with a hug and got misty.

"I feel like I'm sending my son off to kindergarten and shit."

A teary Dr. Cuddles joined the hug. "Me too, boss."

"Look at that face, Cuddles."

"I see it, boss."

"Make us proud, son."

50

A FRAZZLED PERCY made his way to his apartment building. It wasn't until he reached his stairwell until it sank in.

"I'm home."

He dashed up the steps, thinking about how refreshing the shower would be, being able to sleep in his bed for the first time in what seemed like months.

"Daddy's home!"

He opened his door. And froze.

His quarters? Empty.

Couldn't have been Pledgistopheles. They'd parted on good terms. His landlord wasn't in. Had those ant-eating cops Butch and Monty finally caught up to him?

His mind raced with possibilities. Percy knew it could only be the work of one person.

He rushed to the phone and called directory assistance.

"I need the address for Bridget Stanislaw."

51

BRIDGET LIVED IN a Rutger's dorm. How she'd managed to get it didn't matter to Percy. Getting in worried him, until he saw a prime opportunity: a girl taking the walk of shame from the dorm. He rushed in the building past a snoozing security officer straight to the elevator.

Percy knocked on Bridget's apartment door. Waited. He knocked again before forcing his way in. The smell made him retch, a mix of spoiled cottage cheese and bad cabbage.

"Bridget? It's Percy."

Percy looked around. Only one light bulb worked. If flickering for dear life constituted 'working'.

Crumbs abounded. He spied a piece of paper that read "PERCY WINKLER LOAN REPORT." His confusion turned to fear as he noticed his laptop—with a bestiality website on screen—lying on the floor. Next to his open suitcase.

I guess she's not taking any chances with that subject.

Percy put his things back in the suitcase.

"Percy?"

Percy followed the voice.

"Bridget?"

Bridget stumbled out of her bedroom looking more unkempt than ever. Her dreads were filthy. Dirty pimples littered her face. Morsels of food were stuck between her teeth.

"Hey, Percy."

Percy's stomach roiled. Fear of germs, revulsion at Bridge, concern for her well-being all colliding. "You weren't at Pledgistopheles's."

"He couldn't help me. I wasn't internalizing the law."

She staggered toward an unlit room and waved Percy to follow.

He couldn't see shit. His toe knocked against something blunt and hard. He didn't know what it was. Didn't matter. His toe felt afire from the pain. None of that fire illuminated the room. It took the flip of a switch for light to flood in. Roaches scattered from walls littered with pornography, newspaper cutouts, crayon scribbling like "HATE SPEECH IS NOT PROTECTED... REMEMBER THAT, BITCH." "OBSCENITY MUST APPEAL TO PRURIENT INTERESTS."

Bridget waved at the scrawled insanity. "I tried bringing life to the law like Frankenstein, but it wasn't working."

Percy backed up against a charred wall.

Bridget pointed. "See, it isn't arson. True, this is a dwelling, but it's mine. You can't commit arson against your own residence."

"But Bridget—"

"It's not burned, either. Just charred. Therefore, it isn't arson. I've covered most of the bar stuff I had problems with. Commercial Paper was so easy. It's checks, for God's sake."

"Don't you think, you know, that it's a little extreme?"

"Extreme?" Bridget laughed and lurched to a desk.

Percy saw enough. "I'm going to get you some help." He turned to exit.

Percy felt something cold against the back of his head. It was a gun. Tapping against his head knot. Unlike the Syph incident, there wasn't any water dripping from it.

"Percy, I thought about your problems and my problems and found a solution."

"Bridget, you don't have to do this."

"I do, Percy, I do... those are the words required to validate a marriage, I do. Nevertheless, I digress. If you fail, then you lost your morality for nothing."

"How did I lose my morality?"

"You engaged in an unlawful conspiracy just to pass the bar and forced me to enter that conspiracy when I was having problems."

"How did I force you?"

"I didn't want to do this. But you had to pull that little trick with the Uzi."

"That was Syph."

"You were in on it. When she asked how bad I wanted it. You didn't stop her when she solicited me, Percy. After the ride, you encouraged, incited, requested, or otherwise attempted to cause another person, me, to engage in criminal conduct."

"I didn't—"

"Don't apologize, because I wanted it. Moreover, once I accepted, it merged into conspiracy. A conspiracy is an agreement to violate the law. So you're just as guilty as I am."

"I'm not—"

Bridget pistol-whipped him. He fell forward and his head started ringing.

Bridget tapped the gun to her lips. "A co-conspirator is liable for all crimes committed by other co-conspirators in furtherance of the conspiracy. These crimes are, in alphabetical order, arson, assault, battery, false imprisonment. Did I miss any? No." She sighed. "Nevertheless, you can be tried as well. Partner."

With her free hand, Bridget flung a sheet of paper and pen at him.

"I want you to sign this paper."

"Why?"

"I'm listed as a named beneficiary to your estate."

"My estate? I'm broke as a joke."

"I'll take what I can get."

"Are you going to kill me, Bridget?"

"Just sign the paper."

"Don't do this, Bridget."

"It's a win-win. You go to a better place. That's a win for you. I get to take care of my loans. That's a win for me."

"Bridget, I don't—"

She removed the safety. "Sign it."

Percy signed the paper without hesitation. This was how he was going out. Bridget picked up the paper, winced as she read. She pressed the gun to her belly.

"No wonder you failed the bar. They probably couldn't decipher your chicken-scratch handwriting."

Bridget closed her eyes and gathered her thoughts.

"Contracts signed under duress aren't valid. The gun was aimed at you, that's why you signed. Without the threat of bodily harm, you wouldn't have signed." She flopped back on the desk. "I had the hardest time visualizing that." She pressed the gun to her heart. "Thanks, study buddy."

"Study buddy?"

"This." She pointed the gun at the sheet. "I needed someone to sign a contract under duress. And there's no duress like a gun to the head, now is there?" She sucked on the safety.

"You fucking around with me?"

She stopped sucking. "It was either you or my kid sister, but she's a minor. The contract would be revocable on that basis alone."

"Fuck this shit. I'm out."

"You leave and I'll shoot."

"I did what you wanted."

"I have more things to study. So stay. I'll make brownies."

"I'm leaving, Bridget."

"Then I'm shooting."

"It'll be you, Pledgistopheles, or the cops, so what's the difference?"

"For Christ's sake, Percy, don't hold a grudge. I'm just studying for the bar."

Percy snatched his suitcase on the way out.

Bridget waved. "Good luck on the exam."

52

PERCY POUNDED THE empty seat beside him on the train ride home. It hurt like a motherfucker. He couldn't believe the stunt Bridget had pulled. Then again, he wasn't sure how much of it was a stunt. Would she have shot him? She'd pistol-whipped him, after all.

"Son of a bitch!"

The lessons learned from the past week emerged from his subconscious. Her bizarre behavior helped him remember contracts and duress. That was the only thing keeping Percy from calling the cops and ending all of this. He had to ride it out. If he failed, maybe he'd call the cops before Pledgistopheles killed his ass dead for ruining the one hundred percent pass guarantee.

53

WHEN PERCY ARRIVED home, he wasn't sure if he should take a shower.

"What if I need this funk to remember the law?"

Then he realized that if he stayed that funky, they might not let him into the test center. He showered with a test booklet in one hand and Syph's locket around his neck.

He went to bed in boxers and socks. The same, waterlogged test booklet in one hand and Syph's locket in the other.

He drifted to sleep, only to wake up and realize…

"I'm late!"

He grabbed his wallet and keys on the way out of his apartment. Halfway down the block he felt a draft. Looked down. No pants. No shirt. No time to change.

54

PERCY MADE IT BACK to the bar exam. Stressed test-takers packed the testing area. Percy flashed his ticket and took a seat.

Entered beast mode.

Grabbed an exam book.

Broke a pencil on impact.

Sharpened it by gnawing the pencil head.

Resumed the test.

He imagined Pledgistopheles as Jiminy Cricket, guiding him through every fact pattern. Syph appeared as the Ghost of Bar Prep Past, reminding him of his hard-learned lessons. A parade of horrors ensued. Campus cops. Drugs. KFC arson. Everything he'd gone through was on the exam. He worked like a machine until someone tapped his shoulder.

"Hey, Percy."

It was Bridget.

The other test-takers shushed her, so she blew Percy a kiss before taking a seat. Percy grabbed Syph's locket for strength. A few deep breaths were all he needed to get back on track.

The car rides with the Uzi. Hobo's ACL. Uncle's death wish. The shootout. It was all there in Q&As or essay format.

And he was acing it.

Bridget wasn't having such luck. She sneered at her test book.

"Speech," she mumbled. "Public places. Do you have a right?"

Her eyes darted about the room. She was losing it.

"Think. Visualize."

She mimicked Percy's deep breaths, but got the hiccups. She hyperventilated and stood up.

"I have a bomb."

No one cared, so she screamed.

"I have a bomb! I'm gonna use it!"

People were still too busy taking the test.

"Goddamn it! Didn't you hear me?"

A bar proctor with a nametag which read, "BECKY", approached Bridget and said, "Miss?"

Bridget shooed her away. "I have a first amendment right. Freedom of speech."

That roused the test-takers to action.

"Not when you try to incite a crowd!"

"That's right." Bridget smacked her forehead and sat down. She found her groove and resumed her test-taking. Until Becky clutched Bridget's shoulder.

"Come with me, ma'am."

"No, I was just playing."

Becky tightened her grip on Bridget and said, "I don't think you get it. You have to go."

"Get your fucking hands off me!"

Bridget elbowed Becky off her. Becky regained her footing, but Bridget leapt on her like a starving lion on a wounded wildebeest. Becky's training was useless against Bridget's frenzied clawing and mauling.

Once again, nobody cared.

Becky was incapacitated and Bridget hurried to her seat.

"I said I was just playing, bitch. Now where was I?"

Before Bridget could answer a single question on the exam, Becky came from behind and locked her in a rear naked chokehold.

"But *I'm* not playing!" Becky gloated as Bridget tried scratching out of her kung-fu grip.

It was an awesome struggle. Didn't matter to the test-takers. They remained focused on the exam, with a few cast sideways glances.

Percy watched the whole thing, consumed with possibilities. Fearing Bridget would turn her attention to him, he gripped his pencil like a dagger throughout the melee.

Becky didn't let go until Bridget lost consciousness.

Percy worried about Bridget popping up for round two. Until Security dragged Bridget's unconscious ass away.

Becky, always the professional, clutched her swollen jaw and yelled, "Five minutes!"

The test. Percy had completely forgotten. He looked at the remaining questions. All fifty of them. His eyes glazed over fifty empty bubbles on his answer sheet. No way he'd finish in time unless he took drastic measures.

Percy held Syph's locket with one hand and randomly filled empty bubbles on his answer sheet with the other.

Becky clutched her ribs. Mustering enough breath for a hearty call.

"Time! Put your pencils down!"

Percy busily filled each bubble with answer choice A. He wasn't the only one. Other last-minute Marvins followed suit with different random bubble-filling. Some picked a letter like Percy and ran with it. Others used ascending or descending letter patterns. Happy faces. Symbols. Even a middle finger.

Becky stomped like Donkey Kong. "If you don't put your pencils down, you'll be disqualified!"

That was enough for everyone to stop. Everyone except Percy, who still filled out empty bubbles with answer choice A.

Becky wasn't having it.

"Put your pencil down."

He didn't, so Becky snatched his pencil.

Percy pulled out another one and resumed his bubble-filling.

Becky plucked his sheet away and marched off.

Percy leapt from his seat, sprinted behind her, nabbed the sheet, and continued filling in bubbles. Becky tackled him from behind. Security seized his sheet. Percy tried fighting them off, but they dragged him away.

55

PERCY WANDERED the streets. No missions from Pledgistopheles. Bar already taken. Feeling empty. The past weekend had built him up for one purpose.

The test.

With no results for three months, he wasn't sure what to do with himself. If he'd failed, Pledgistopheles would have his ass. Pretty much meant these could be the last three months of his life.

Percy decided to go out on top. Withdraw all his money and live it up.

Percy rushed to the nearest ATM.

His balance? -$23,999.

"Pledgistopheles?"

So much for the payment plan.

56

PERCY RESUMED HIS LIFE, waiting tables.

The night of the exam results, he visited the Bar website, gripping Syph's locket, frantically looking for his name among the passed under the letter W.

He wasn't listed.

"Pledgistopheles."

Failure meant death.

Percy didn't know if he should go to the cops. But what would he say? And would they believe him? Would they be on Pledgistopheles's payroll?

Maybe the goons were on their way to him. Right now.

A familiar voice said, "Fonzie?"

It was Pledgistopheles. Dressed in a suit.

Percy swallowed hard. "How'd you—"

"The door was open." He screwed up his face while scoping the room. "Let's go to the living room."

Percy took a deep breath and followed Pledgistopheles.

"Take a seat, Fonzie."

"Take a seat? For what?"

Pledgistopheles stuffed a hand inside his suit jacket.

He's gonna shoot me.

Pledgistopheles gripped something that bulged through the fabric.

Goddamn it. He's gonna shoot me.

"Do I really have to sit?"

"It'll be easier that way."

Percy didn't feel like arguing. He was fucked and might as well take it sitting down.

So he sat down. Gingerly. Carefully. Nervously.

Pledgistopheles pulled it out.

Percy closed his eyes, clenching his teeth and fists.

He felt something light on his lap. Opened his eyes. "A stuffed envelope."

Pledgistopheles pointed at it. "Read it."

Percy squinted his eyes as he read. "A letter from the New York Bar?"

Pledgistopheles stared.

"Mr. Winkler, we detected a grading mistake on the multistate portion of your exam. Our integrity requires that we fix that which is not right. You have, in fact, passed the bar exam taken last year, making your recent test unnecessary. Please disregard any prior notice of failure and accept our humble apology for any undue pain we regretfully caused you."

Percy leaned back. "This can't be true."

"Check your computer."

Percy ran to his room. Plopped in front of his computer. "My name isn't there."

Pledgistopheles pointed at the screen. "Refresh that bitch."

Percy hit refresh.

His name. Listed among those who passed.

"This a trick?"

"You passed."

"I passed." It hit him. "I passed." After all this time. All the trials and tribulations. "I passed."

"Now you can get back to your life."

"Get back to my life? I saw people murdered."

"No, you didn't."

"Syph died in my arms."

Pledgistopheles's eyes bugged out. "You better tell her that." He pulled out a gun.

Percy turned and wished he had a gun. All he could do? Smile. Tentatively, but building to barking laughter at the shooter.

A bloody Syph.

She pointed her own gun. Fired recklessly.

Percy leapt out of the way. She set her aim on Pledgistopheles and unloaded a number of rounds into his chest. Blood oozed everywhere as his body violently shook.

Syph croaked, "Where... is... my locket?"

She staggered to Percy.

"We know... you has it. We... wants it back."

Percy's hands quivered. He fumbled to remove the locket from his neck.

Syph engulfed him. Blood dripped from her fingers as she gripped at the locket. Frenzied, failed gripping. Percy tried helping, but she slapped his hands away. Syph finally wrangled it from him. Cooed like Gollum. "That's my precious." She perversely stroked her precious, I mean locket. Over and over again.

Syph stalked Percy. He staggered back.

Her lips pulled taut. Blood dripped from her gums, between the gaps in her teeth. Percy fell to the ground. Syph leaned in.

Nose to nose, she kissed him. "Thanks, homie."

Pledgistopheles sat up and barked, "Are you fucking done?"

Syph waved him away. "Give me another minute."

"Another minute? For what? More melodramatic bullshit?"

"I have no idea what you're talking about."

"You sure you don't, 'Syph'?"

He wounded her.

"First you get all Karla Marx with Trent, and now you're doing *Lord of the Rings*?"

Syph's shoulders dropped. Her bottom lip drooped.

"Tell me you didn't quote Obi Wan during your death speech again."

"I didn't."

"Good."

"I quoted Yoda."

"Jesus."

"You don't understand. It was good."

Pledgistopheles busily pulled packets of red goop from under his clothes. "Fucking hate this part."

Syph raised a bloody finger. "I told him, 'Do. There is no try.'"

"Get the fuck outta here."

She left the apartment. And returned seconds later. "May the force—"

"I'm gonna force you—" Pledgistopheles hurled a blood packet that narrowly missed her.

"Yoda."

Percy raised his hands and swatted the air, warding off everything.

Pledgistopheles warded off more fake blood. "As I was about to say. None of your classmates died. It was all special effects. Just like this shooting we just put together with Miss Baby Mama Drama.'

"So I didn't commit any crimes?"

"Oh, the crimes were real. Shit work that nobody wanted to do, distractions to cover up our cross-town operations, and other shit we thought would be funny."

"What?"

"Look at it as pro bono work to benefit a small, family business. Granted, you paid for it, but you helped out a few struggling actors like Trent, Kent, Michelle—aka Syph…"

"What about Bridget?"

"What about her?"

"Was she real?"

"She sure was real. A real piece of shit. Fuck her and Harvard Law. They're cut off."

"I should've failed. I saw them throw away my answers and… did I really pass or was I passed because you… you know…"

"Does it matter?"

"I can't believe this."

"If denial floats your boat, go right ahead."

"I'm a wreck. An absolute wreck."

"Not a surprise. Not a surprise at all. For you, my friend, psychiatric counseling is on the house. What do you think about that, tough guy?"

"What do I think about that? After you bled my bank account dry, I'm broke and need a job."

"Fuggetaboutit."

57

INSIDE PLEDGISTOPHELES'S frat house, a new batch of nerds in black robes, gaudy gold necklaces, and powdered wigs on their heads were jostled awake.

Some of the geeks were Trent, Stranger, and Kent acting undercover. They exchanged knowing glances. The door opened. Pledgistopheles marched in with a remote control.

"All of you retards are here for one reason: You can't pass the bar. You did it your way and failed... miserably. So now? We do it," he started singing, "my way..."

Some geeks pled, whimpered, or cried for mercy. Trent, unbeknownst to the geeks, gestured to Pledgistopheles.

"Fuck this."

Trent made a mad dash for the door. Pledgistopheles pressed the remote control. The gold chain around Trent's neck hummed. The chain started smoking as Trent feigned death by electrocution.

Pledgistopheles stood triumphant. "Anybody else wanna leave?"

Nope.

"We're gonna do a little criminal law cram session."

A wimpy voice shouted, "Oh no!"

Pledgistopheles continued, "Every night, you get a bag."

The voice grew louder. "Oh no! No, oh no!"

A pissed Syph tried getting the whiner's attention. It was Percy.

She whispered, "You're overdoing it."

"Sorry," he whispered back.

"In the bag you'll find a job you gotta do. You don't do the jobs? You die. You snitch? You die. You get locked up? You die. Capisce?"

Percy started crying. "I don't wanna die."

Pledgistopheles repeated, "Capisce?"

Percy whined to another geek, "We'd better do what he says."

The geek agreed.

Pledgistopheles stomped in place. "Capisce?"

Syph elbowed Percy, who finally got it.

"Oh, sorry."

Then, as if channeling Robbie the Robot, he recited, "How do we learn by doing 'jobs'?" Percy flashed a goofy grin.

His terrible acting job horrified Pledgistopheles.

"This is gonna be a long weekend."

SAMPLE CHAPTER
TONTO CANTO POCAHONTAS
AVAILABLE NOW

MY MOTHER SET ME UP to visit a Wyoming tribe with a name she couldn't pronounce.

"The name doesn't matter, boy. They need men."

She met a woman from the tribe ten years ago at a powwow, tall and exotic, named Gertie, and as archaic as her manners. "They don't make women like that anymore, Crispy. She's not ruined by all this modern stuff. Gertie is a nice, traditional woman. I sent her an overnight letter, since she doesn't have a phone. Had the messenger wait for her reply and send it to me. And guess what? Gertie is available."

"You want me to marry her?"

"No, boy. She has daughters. Single, unmarried daughters. Three of them. They're so desperate for men to replenish the tribe, I'm sure at least one would find you passable enough."

Didn't know whether to thank my mother or take offense. Not that it mattered. The trip was set.

On the plane, I asked the flight attendant if the meal had nuts or shellfish, given my allergies. She gave me a puzzled look and scurried to the back. When she came around, she asked me, "Are you a Hebrew?"

Turtle Rock, in the northeast portion of Wyoming, had a population of two hundred. The indigenous population was twenty-five percent there, as opposed to one percent nationally. Europeans there for 250 years. Dust there since the dawn of man, and it found its way into everything. Within an hour of arriving, my white shirt turned off-white. Skin all chalky. Grains in my mouth. Wearing shoes and socks didn't stop pebbles finding a home between my toes.

Sun straight down ruining your skin. People looked leathery. As if somebody mated with a handbag back in the day. A van picked me up. Flat lands stretched out with nothing but rocks and boulders. Cars drove ten miles under the speed limit. No rush, because there wasn't anything rush-worthy. It took forever to get to my destination.

The driver dropped me off in front of a small ranch home. Not another abode in sight. The door was open. I knocked anyway. Said, "Hello. It's Crispy."

No answer, so I walked in, repeated my greeting. Silence answered.

It was one room with a kitchenette, television, and couch. No phone, no photos, no evidence of life, much less daughters. Maybe I had the wrong house? My cell phone had no bars. Still, I walked around with it skyward, like Mr. Spock testing the air on a strange alien planet. I went outside. Roamed and found no sign of anything, just like my trip there.

Back inside, I took a seat and stared at the television. Gertie didn't show until nightfall.

Wish she never showed.

Gertie was a Native who looked older than my grandmother. I thought nothing of it, figuring she was harmless. I said, "Glad to meet you."

She eyefucked me. Weird, but they had a man shortage, after all.

I asked, "Your daughters are still out?"

"Yep."

She went to her car and returned with her "daughters." Three cats.

I laughed. "I meant your real daughters."

She laughed too. "You hungry?"

"I'm allergic."

"To food?"

"To cats."

She stared at me. I sneezed. She cackled. Whipped out a can of beans and burned them in a pot.

What kind of hellhole was this place? Gertie's old ass. Burned beans. Cats. I had to get out of there. But how? The cats made me cough.

The cats.

My excuse.

Gertie scraped and scooped beans from the pot to a bowl. I said, "Thanks for your hospitality. The last kind of guest I would want to be is one who imposed. Especially to a graceful hostess such as yourself."

She scratched her cooch.

I continued, "It's my allergies to cats. Which means I can't stay here. Sorry. It's been brief, but great."

Gertie rounded up the cats, one by one, and tossed them out. Slammed the door on them. Resumed scraping gummy, burnt beans from her pot.

Like the beans, I was stuck, only with no one to scrape me out. I had a week until my scheduled flight back.

*   *   *

AFTER "DINNER," I STEPPED OUT, considering taking a walk. Heard some horrid creature growl and reconsidered the walk. Went inside and turned on the television. Two channels worked. I figured boredom was a hell of a lot better than whatever beasts roamed outside. Until Gertie surfaced.

Wearing a towel, she stood right between me and the television. Started stretching. Then did yoga. Ass in the air. My air, to be specific. The towel hiked up her thigh. To her unmentionables. I saw it all. And could not unsee what I saw when she spread her cheeks.

A hemorrhoid the size of a plum poked out. Said hello. And introduced her friends.

Gertie said, "Can you help me apply my ointment?"

I channeled my inner wooden Indian. Furrowed brow. Constipated expression. Unmoving.

She repeated herself and I made a snoring noise. She stared. I snored.

She took a seat and turned to the worst possible movie. One that would blow my cover. *The Big Lebowski*. I loved it a little too much. Couldn't watch without reciting lines, or busting out laughing. My life was in my hands. And that gave me no comfort.

But I sat. Eyes open. Watching. Snoring.

Everyone knows the drill when holding back a laugh. You close your mouth. Tighten your lips. Last thing you do is open your mouth. Problem for me? I had to fake snoring while keeping in a laugh. I was fine when they peed on The Dude's rug, and got through every time Walter told Donnie to shut the fuck up. But when they threatened to cut off The Dude's johnson? I lost it.

Whimpering giggles turned to frenetic hyena laughing. I couldn't take it. I lost the fight, so I made flight to my bedroom.

The next day, I told her I slept with my eyes open.

She asked, "Why was ya walkin' around, then?"

"I sleepwalk. With my eyes open."

Gertie had never experienced anything like it. "You was laughin' at the television."

"No. I was ... laughing at ... my dreams. My dreams. Yes, laughing at my dreams."

"You was laughin' at all them dong jokes on the television."

"No, it just seemed like I was laughing at those dong jokes on television. But I wasn't. I was sleepwalking, after all."

"Oblivious to the world?"

"Yes. Completely oblivious. To the world."

"No matter what you heard. Or what you felt?"

Didn't like what she implied. I imagined her rubbing those horrid hemorrhoids on me. It ended my sleepwalking. Instead, I planned to stay in my room. Blame it on sleeping sickness, which afflicted members of my tribe and made me prone to violent knife fights.

I told her my plight.

Gertie bugged. "The hell am I to do?"

"Lock me in my room. For your own safety."

"What if you need a piss?"

I grabbed a bucket. "Piss bucket."

I didn't trust her. I locked my door and lodged the bed against the doorknob. Protecting my knob from Gertie.

What was my mother thinking by having me stay with Gertie? Her idea of a joke? Maybe a trick? Yes. I'd be forced to find refuge with a buxom young maiden. Yes, that was probably it. Just weather the Gertie storm for a rainbow to come from the skies, leading me to a pot of pussy gold and Lucky Charms doing a jig. Don't believe it? Me either. What choice did I have but ride it out? Grind it out. Without Gertie grinding on me.

*   *   *

THAT AFTERNOON WE DROVE her busted-ass Rez car to the nearest town.

She did the driving. Chugging, to be exact. The car shook, smoked, stopped, dripped. It was the first time in my life I actually wished a cop would stop and ticket a car I rode. If po-po came a calling, I'd tell him I was a hostage. Hopefully it would be a female officer. Hot. Native. Tribal officer. Wearing those tight-ass pants. All sexed up like the one in that Chili Peppers song *Sir Psycho Sexy*. If she tried to "Rodney King" Gertie, I'd appeal to her tender side.

Unfortunately, we made it to our destination without police intervention.

It was a lone restaurant on a barren strip with a *Texas Chainsaw Massacre* vibe. Reminded me why I hated the boonies. I saw *The Twilight Zone* and *Blue Velvet*, so I knew quiet, remote places hid creepiness. *Twin Peaks*-level freaky-deaky shit. Like Agent Cooper stuck in the Black Lodge, there was no getting the fuck out of Dodge. I was broke. No credit cards, no cash. Everything was supposed to be handled.

I was handled. In a good way, for once, as soon as we entered the restaurant.

Streamers and all kinds of birthday stuff abounded.

I asked Gertie, "Who is the birthday for?"

She said, "My niece."

Niece? She pointed at an eight-year-old.

Yep. Sold the wrong bill of goods.

I took a plate and loaded it up, hoping to find a honey I

could sit next to. No chance for romance, since everyone wore wedding bands. At least, everyone of legal age but Gertie. As far as their husbands? There was one dude for every five women. Even then, I couldn't assume all the guys were husbands. They could've been brothers, or uncles. There weren't any public displays of affection, so I couldn't tell who was a couple.

Everyone buried their heads in their plates, chowing down like they were starving. Burping, farting, burping while farting. I couldn't get a word in. Soon as I started talking, someone ripped out a big one. Of all the tribes I'd been around, never had I seen such shitty manners.

Gertie scored some weed from the busboy. Offered me a hit. I passed. She replied, "Guess that means more for me." She got wasted on straight gin shots and used me as a living crutch, ambling her to the bar, to the food, to the bathroom. To her car. I drove us home while she sang show tunes in the back seat.

Or at least, tried driving her home.

I got lost. Pulled over by a cop. Male cop, unfortunately, who knew Gertie and offered to guide me back to her place. I complied. We helped her into bed.

I asked, "Is she going to be okay?"

"She'll sleep the night and wake up better rested than you or me."

Before he left, I thought about taking full advantage of Gertie's unconscious state. Leaving her in her bedroom and enjoying my first night of peace. Watching television, stretching my legs, using the toilet. No need for the piss bucket. A glimmer of paradise in hell.

Reality struck. The cop could be my Charon, delivering me across the river Styx, out of Hades. I wondered if there were other women from Gertie's tribe I didn't know about. Younger women. Single, younger women. I wasn't about to risk it. Like Lot, I needed to escape before being fucked in the ass. No looking back or I'd be turned a salt lick for Gertie.

I said, "Officer, Gertie was supposed to drive me to the airport tonight."

"At this hour?"

"I have a redeye flight."

"She's in no condition to drive."

"Yes, sir. And I can't take her car. I don't have money for transportation. Could you give me a ride?"

I had my ticket on the counter, my departure date circled in red on a calendar, and a Post-It on the refrigerator. If he looked at any of these, I'd be busted.

Now he was Orpheus. I was Eurydice. I thought, "Don't look, motherfucker. Don't look. Or I'll be trapped in Hades."

He said, "Sure. Get your things."

Grabbing my things, I rolled out with a quickness you wouldn't believe.

The cop drove me to the airport. The closer we got, the more I felt like Han Solo, escaping an asteroid that turned out to be a giant space slug. The closer to the airport, the closer I was to escaping the jaws of the monster. Closer—through the throat, teeth closing, closing—until we made it out.

The cop dropped me off. I was free.

Trapped in an airport all night? Sleeping on a hard, plastic chair with no pillow? Cold from overactive air-conditioning with no blanket? Think that's bad? I got two words for you.

Piss bucket.

'Nuff said.

The next morning I had my ticket adjusted. I was bound for New York.

*   *   *

I EXPECTED MY MOTHER to rip into me, disappointed by my failure to stay and weather Hurricane Gertie.

She wasn't.

Turns out the inbreeding documentary lost relevance.

My mother said, "We were both tricked, Crispy. Gertie lied. So did the documentary. So I'm glad you didn't end up getting anyone pregnant."

"Was there a rebuttal? Or maybe an exposé on the documentary's veracity?"

"Sure was. Turns out it was done by Germans."

"The rebuttal?"

"No."

"The exposé?"

"No. The documentary itself. It was done by Germans."

"And?"

"And, what?"

"And there was no exposé? No repudiation of the science?"

"Didn't you hear me? The documentary was done by Germans. That's all I, you or any of our people need to hear. Now look, son, while you were gallivanting in Wyoming, your cousin Daisy found someone. Just like that. So she's off the market. Maybe you should transfer to UVA—and not be such a stranger to your community."

"Ma, with you and Opie, I can never be a stranger."

"I can only do so much for you, son. These ladies aren't getting any younger. And you don't have much longer to find a woman."

Thank you for reading CHUMPED COLLECTION.

I know your time is valuable and I sincerely thank you for finishing this story. If you would take a brief moment to return to where you purchased the book and leave a review, it would be much appreciated.

Reviews help new readers find my work and accurately decide if the book is for them as well as provide feedback for my future writing.

Also please visit http://alexeiauld.com/updates.html to register for updates and future releases.

ABOUT THE AUTHOR

Alexei Auld is an Off-Rez alum of Sundance's Native Writing Workshop and Columbia Law School. His writing has been featured in E! True Hollywood Story, Fondo Del Sol, and numerous curated festivals and publications.

www.ingramcontent.com/pod-product-compliance
Lightning Source LLC
Chambersburg PA
CBHW020618180626
46810CB00007B/2838